The Cad RedDot

Books by Kee Briggs

The Third Removed
The Painted War
Finders-Keepers
Losers-Weepers
The Painted Lady
A Few Good Old Men

The Usher Orlop Mysteries

The Golden Janus/The Pewter Masks
The Nickel Trophy/The Bronze Bones
The Brass Porttaits/The Zinc Ormolu
The Silver Scepter/The Rhodium Dragon
The Copper Shakes

The Sage Grayling Mysteries

The Yellow Ochre Stain
Lamp Blzck Pit

The Asti Fsntasies

Charm Catcher/Dream Weaver

ebook

Write To Live Longer

The Cad Red Dot

A Sage Grayling Mystery
#3

Kee Briggs

Keescapes Publishing
Satellite Beach, Florida

The Cad Red Dot

Copyright © 2011 by Kee Briggs

Keescapes Publishing books may be ordered through
booksellers or by contacting:

Keescapes Publishing

90 Flamingo Dr.

Satellite Beach, FL 32937

www.keescapes.com

KeescapesPublishing@gmail.com

ISBN 978-0-9820044-7-0

Published in the United States of America

The Cad Red Dot

Kee Briggs

Chapter 1

—⟋ɯ⟍—

Sage sat across a glass-topped patio table from his new client. A lucrative, signed contract for an extensive Trompe-L'Oeil painting had been shoved aside to make room for coffee mugs. Sage was idly surveying the two pairs of cowboy boots under the table. Sage's were highly polished dress boots with two-inch heels to add even more authority to his 6'4" slender frame. In contrast, Snapper Keel was shod in scuffed work-boots with run-over heels. They seemed rather incongruous with their owner's obvious wealth.

"The sun will hit the dining room wall in another twenty minutes," said Keel. "This is a typical Florida day, so you'll see what I'm talking about when I say, 'sub-tropic light'. Tomorrow afternoon, I'll take you out to the ranch house so you can see the light there."

The two men were sitting on a 5th floor balcony overlooking the Banana River in Cocoa Beach, Florida. Nearly the whole wall was glass sliders. Sage glanced through the glass wall of the living room to the elevated dining room, where he would be painting the three walls. Keel had relocated the kitchen door to correspond to the position of the back door at the ranch house where he'd been born and spent his entire life. Recently he'd bought this penthouse condo and turned the family ranch over to his grandson.

"Is the ranch house occupied?"

"No. I built a new house for my daughter-in-law when my son

was killed in Viet Nam. Mikey, my grandson grew up on the ranch, but he had to be a Marine like his father. Now he's retired and I can finally shed the responsibility of the whole thing. I wanted to give it to my son decades ago. Mikey just built a fancy house on the other side of the ranch nearer civilization."

"How's your schedule. Are there any dates I'll have to work around?"

Nothing of any importance. If something comes up, I'll do it elsewhere until you're finished."

"I'll take my ranch photos tomorrow. I use a digital camera so I can make prints at a drugstore. I want you to tell me if there is anything you want changed. If something is to be added, I'll have to see it. We can compare the new shots with the old black and white photos. Once the scene is set, I'll return to Albuquerque to make the cartoons and collect materials and equipment. That will take a couple of weeks. Then I'll drive back here."

"I'll be coming and going. Sometimes I spend the night in the old ranch house. I'll give you the condo keys and the front entry code. I have two parking spaces in the garage. I'll clear one for you. Use the front bedroom and bath. The kitchen is all yours as long as you don't leave a mess. I eat out most of the time."

"I'm what you might call a microwave chef. When I'm working, I don't like having to clean up to go out. It wastes too much time and it breaks my concentration. I usually exist on microwave dinners while I'm working."

Keel checked the dining room again. "Now you can see the quality of the light." He swung around to look at the setting sun. "We're in a red flag fire watch. It has been far too dry. The chance of brush fires is extremely high. If too much smoke gets into the air, the light changes."

****

Sage spent the morning walking along the ocean beach. At noon he met Keel for lunch at the Surf, one of the old time restaurants and watering holes. Keel was well known by the staff, who showed him considerable deference. Sage passed on the offer of a gator tail appetizer, opting for Pompano en Papillote.

"When we finish lunch, we'll head for the ranch. I hope the smoke doesn't interfere with the lighting. There are fires in several areas."

"Smoke lends more red to the spectrum. If necessary I can make adjustments."

"Before you take any pictures I'd better do a little housecleaning, like picking up dirty shorts and socks."

"If you find anything you don't want in the painting, just tell me and I'll hit the delete button."

Keel wasn't sufficiently computer literate to get the joke.

During the drive to Osceola County, Keel gave a running history lesson on the territory along their route. They left the main arterial, turning onto a secondary road. After several miles, Keel swept his hand vaguely toward the front and right of the Jeep. "That's my land." When they finally turned onto a dirt trail, there was no development in sight. "We're on my land now. The old ranch buildings are back in a ways and over a rise by a lake."

"This is what I call privacy. Where are the other houses?"

"They're clear on the other side, off a paved road where they can get electricity and mail service. It's a long way around by road. There's too much water to cross by car unless you know where to go. And it's a fair piece by horse."

When Keel's Jeep crested a rise, a scene out of the old west presented itself, complete with a hitching rail by the front porch. Behind the house was a scattering of outbuildings, a large barn, and many corrals. The layout may have been generations old, but everything was in prime condition.

Keel stopped on top of the rise to silently survey the scene for a moment. There was a little hitch in his voice as he said, "I was born in that house, as was my son. Things are winding down for me. When I'm gone, this old place won't even be a memory to anyone."

As Sage's eyes swept over the ranch yard, he felt the same tingling along the back of his neck he'd felt when he first sighted the ruins of the Hacienda in Albuquerque. There was a real chunk of history spread out before him. Keel was right. With no one left to tend it, even the memory would be lost.

"With your permission, I'd like to perpetuate the memories a little longer. You know the kind of painting I do. There are probably hundreds of scenes and vignettes around here to tickle the fancy of yet unborn generations. I'd like to record as many as I can for future paintings."

Keel turned to face his young companion. "I'd like that. After I'm gone this will fall into ruin. That's a rapid process in this climate."

"When I come back, I'll bring before and after shots of my place. You'll see why I honor old things."

Keel slipped the vehicle into gear and moved down to the ranch house. He parked over to the side. "Don't want any reflections off this thing to mess up the light coming in through the front window."

Sage stepped back to take a picture with his Elph of the front of what he had learned was a saddlebag house. The original house was one large room with a fireplace on the right side. Later, an equal number of square feet were added on the other side of the fireplace wall. The addition had been divided into two bedrooms.

"It isn't quite like it used to be. That little lean-to on the left is a bathroom. There's a sink in the kitchen. The bunkhouse has a bathroom too. I put in a gas pump in the brush, up the hill, to fill a big tank. I don't like to listen to a generator, so there's no electricity."

Keel stepped up onto the porch to unlock a padlock. "After the Indian threat was over, this door was never locked until about ten years ago. Now everything has to be under lock and key. There's a spare key hanging on the nail under that cow skull." Keel swung the door open and extended his hand. "There's your subject."

Sage had already seen the old black and white photos that he was supposed to use for the painting. Now he was to get the color references.

Keel pulled up a blind that covered the front window, admitting the blazing afternoon sun, setting the highlights and shadows that Sage would be using. Keel rolled up a blind over the rear window, exposing the scene the artist would show in his painted window.

Sage moved about the room taking reference shots of details and the interior colors. When he turned his attention to the scene from the window, he said, "Pick the position where you get the scene you want to record."

Keel moved back and forth until he said, "This is it."

Sage took over Keel's spot and stooped down enough to duplicate the shorter man's view before shooting a series of pictures.

"Do you want the door open so you can see more of the outside?"

"No. See all those marks on the door?"

There were lines and numbers on all of the verticals that made up the door.

"Yes."

"I want you to put those in the painting. On each birthday, the height of each kid born in this house was recorded. The last marks on the right are those of my son. The next ones are mine."

It took some time to make certain he had an accurate recording of the family history. By that time the sun was dropping behind the hill.

In the failing light, Keel headed back to Cocoa Beach. After making an appointment for 10:00 the next morning, he let Sage off in the condo parking lot by his rental car.

A few blocks north was a Walgreens where Sage availed himself of the digital photo processing machine. He had a full set of colored pictures in hand before hunting for a dining spot.

When Sage arrived for his morning appointment, Keel had laid out all his old photographs, which showed the interior that Sage was to depict, plus photos showing the ranch yard as it was in earlier times.

It took the rest of the morning to decide viewpoints and what to include. Ultimately, the old slab dining table with its benches and a large hand-built armchair with an Indian blanket thrown across it were the only free-standing objects that were not lined up against the wall.

As Sage put all of the faded, old black and white photos and his new color prints into a manila envelope, he said "I'll be back in a couple/three weeks ready to start painting. This will be an interesting challenge. Normally, a Trompe-L'Oeil painting is constructed to be read from a single viewpoint. In this case, the primary view is to be from the living room, but I don't want it to fall apart when seen from the dining room table."

"I'm anxious to add my personal touch to this cold, sterile hunk of masonry. I don't know how people can enjoy life in one of these cliff dwellings. I'll be awaiting your return."

Fortified by a fat deposit check in his hip pocket, Sage pointed his rental car toward Orlando for his return flight the next morning to Albuquerque.

Chapter 2

Sage made his ritualistic circuit of the Hacienda in his classic 1982 Cadillac Seville Elegante, named Dreadnought, before pulling into the garage. The Hacienda was west of Albuquerque, too far from the river and too close to the Indian reservation for the location to be high on the schedule for developer acquisition. Sage had a penchant for poking around in out-of-the-way places. One day he was investigating an old, overgrown track off a county road and came on the shell of an ancient Mexican hacienda building hidden in the brush. The three-foot thick, soft brick walls were still standing, but time and insects had destroyed the vigas....beams. All the flat tile roofs had fallen in.

Sage's creative eye had built the image of the most magnificent Trompe-L'Oeil studio that had ever existed.

With an enormous investment in faith and sweat-equity, Sage contracted to buy the property and began the long, slow process of resurrection. He worked through many seasonal cycles until he had a partially habitable structure. There was still much work to be done, but now he could flirt with the sin of pride. His dream was being transformed into reality. It was becoming an object of envy even by those without Sage's creative vision.

The Hacienda was a rectangular, approximately 100x170 foot

structure of stucco over brick. The walls were 22 feet high and periodically pierced by narrow windows, which were protected on the inside by heavy mesquite shutters and on the exterior by burglar bars. The east-facing front entry was a pair of heavy mesquite doors large enough to admit a small truck. A pedestrian door in one of the great doors permitted human entry into a covered passage-way through to the jardin....garden. The sala or living room was on the left. Some recent affluence had permitted Sage to divide the old 40-foot-long room into the sala in front and dining room behind. He also had been able to furnish the newly renovated space.

Behind the dining room was the old Mexican kitchen with its line of brazier arches. Sage had decked over the holes on top and added a phalanx of small, white appliances led by a pair of high-powered microwave ovens. Beyond the kitchen were pantry rooms and an exit into the walled-in family garden area.

Across the entryway from the new sala was the old one. The recent construction project had created a large sitting room with four oversized wardrobe closets fitted with bi-fold doors. Inside each was a set of built-in bunk beds. Sage could handle up to eight overnight guests, but his accommodations were not sufficiently commodious to encourage any long-term stays.

His greatest pride was the 20x100 foot studio with 18-foot ceilings. Now, that was a studio.

At the west end of the studio was a glass wall separating Sage's private living quarters, complete with king-sized bed, fireplace, leather easy chairs, computer/office space, wet bar and two spacious walk-in closets. Between the closets was a door into Sage's notorious bathroom. At one time, an enterprising individual attempted to turn the Hacienda into a school. Boys' and girls' bathrooms had been constructed in a former bedroom. Sage had turned the girls' side into his wet bar and closets. The boys' side was still pretty much as it had been. There were four doorless commode stalls on the south wall, four urinals and four shower heads along the north wall and four wash basins along the baffle wall behind the entry to the jardin. Sage had added a laundry to the facility. He'd also put a outer door on the bathroom to make heating possible when needed.

The garage was the sole deviation from the original footprint. He added an oversized double-car, fake adobe structure to the east side of the Hacienda. A kitchen window became the connecting door to the house.

On the kitchen table was a small pile of mail that had been collected by his potter tenant, Tinna. When he'd taken his turn around the Hacienda, he'd noticed her old flatbed truck was missing. He'd tooted his horn in case she was at her pottery back behind the main house. If she didn't show up in a few minutes, it was probable that she was out on a supply run.

Sage toted his bag and art kit across the jardin into his personal living area. He dropped the bag on the bed and the kit on a drafting table before heading back to the kitchen. He'd had a snack on the plane, which had not compensated for missing lunch. After rummaging around in the freezer, he settled on a chicken pot pie. He didn't want to overeat this late in the afternoon and mess up dinner.

"¡Oje, Cabron!" The lusty call came from the back door. When it banged open, much of the sunlight was blotted out by a 6'2" full-bodied blonde female who habitually wore 2" heeled cowboy boots so she could look Sage straight in the eye. Her abundant chest was continually turning male heads.

Tinna swooped into the kitchen to envelope Sage in an exuberant hug and to plant a hearty kiss on his cheek. Sage returned the demonstration in kind.

"How was your trip? Did you get the commission?"

"The plane didn't crash and I have the commission. It's much bigger than I had anticipated. It involves three walls of a dining room. It will create some interesting perspective problems. What's been happening around here?"

"I'm unloading the last ana gama firing, which came out beautifully. My problem is no longer production, but marketing. My galleries are trying to demand exclusive rights in too large an area."

"You're complaining because you are becoming such a hot commodity?"

"I'm no commodity," declared the indignant potter.

Sage smiled as he let his eyes slowly trail down the tall, curvaceous form, detouring as attractions dictated. "Why do the galleries all want to do photo displays of you in conjunction with your ceramics display?"

"That's just marketing."

"Yeah, that's what I said..."

"Pinche Cabron."

Tinna swore like a trooper, but always in a foreign language in an attempt to avoid some of the social pitfalls associated with having a foul mouth.

Sage broke off the verbal confrontation by asking, "Do you want one of these to hold you over until we can go into town for dinner? We'll celebrate my new commission."

"Okay. Can we go somewhere that serves fish? I'm getting tired of eating those legged things."

****

It had been an enjoyable evening. Tinna had gotten her fill of fish. Sage was pleased with his prime rib and Yorkshire pudding. Dreadnought was gliding down the road. Soft music was playing in the background.

When the news came on, Sage cocked an ear to follow the brushfire report from central Florida. Suddenly, he became alert when the reporter announced that as a result of an Osceola County fire, what appeared to be a number of unmarked graves had been exposed on the Circle K ranch. The announcer continued to say that the authorities were planning on questioning the owner of the property to find out who was buried there.

"The Circle K. That's Keel's ranch," said Sage, as he jammed down on the accelerator. Dreadnought responded as per expectation.

By the time they reached the den TV set, the networks were back into regular programming and the cable channels were recycling. Sage was in deep thought as he mixed drinks.

Not being one who savored silence, Tinna said, "That shouldn't affect your commission, should it?"

"I wouldn't think so. For as long as that place has been inhabited, there are probably lots of people buried on that ranch. I imagine there are several generations of Keels buried on that property."

"Are you going to call your client?"

"Not now. We don't know anything about it. If there is a story behind it, someone will let us know all about it very quickly. I don't like things rocking the boat before I start on a project. It's easy for the client to cancel. I'm covered because of the way my contract reads. There was a substantial down payment. However, I'd rather have the job than collect the penalty for cancellation. This looks like a fun job in color tones I like. In my off moments, I have permission to poke around the ranch house. There's a lifetime of good material there for a painter."

When the cable channel again reported on the top news stories, there wasn't much more information available than there had been over the radio. As a fire crew was moving through a burned out area, a vehicle tire had popped a human skull out of a slight depression in the ground. Further investigation showed a dozen similar depressions that were lined up side-by-side along a slight rise in a generally marshy area. A fire fighter sank his Pulaski tool into a couple more depressions and exposed additional bones. The fire fighters withdrew and called the sheriff.

The report repeated the information that the find had been made on the Circle K ranch and that the authorities wished to talk with the owner to see if that was an unmarked cemetery.

The newscaster apologized for not have video coverage because the site was far into private property and in an area without road access. The nearby fire was producing too much smoke for the local news helicopter to get any photos before dark.

"That's not sounding as if it's a cemetery," commented Tinna.

"It appears that there will be no further information until tomorrow. I'm going to continue to work on my cartoon. Time is getting short before I want to leave."

For the next couple of days, bits and pieces of information were being dribbled out by the Osceola Sheriff and States Attorney. The property owner, Snapper Keel, denied any knowledge of the burial site as did his grandson, Michael Keel, who had recently assumed ranch operations.

Sage decided that it was time to call his client to make sure the job was still on. His first attempt failed. There was no answering machine where he could leave a message.

Sage spent the morning in his studio working on the cartoon. Periodically he'd take a break and make a call.

When he finally made contact, he said, "Hi, Snapper. This is Sage. I thought I'd better check in. I've been hearing reports on TV. I was wondering if there was any change in plans."

"No. As far as I am concerned everything is still 'go'. There's a lot of fuss, but I know absolutely nothing about those graves. They are directly across the lake from the ranch house. The detective from the sheriff's office keeps wanting to talk to me but he's awful stingy with information. Rumors have it that the first grave is pretty fresh and as you go down the line they get progressively older."

"How fresh is fresh?"

"They're not saying yet. I did find out that archaeologists have been called in to excavate the site. The crime scene boys got too heavy handed. They didn't come up with much useable information outside of the skeleton itself."

"I'll be finished up here in a week and then I'll start moving in your direction."

"Good. Give me a call when you get close so we can make arrangements to meet at the condo."

Sage became a perpetual motion machine. He had to finish his cartoon, resupply his art kit when a new shipment of oil paints finally arrived, have Dreadnought serviced, load ladders and ramps and put money aside for Tinna to pay bills. Life was a lot easier with Tinna around while he was away on a long commission.

When Sage was still a few hours from Cocoa Beach, he began calling Keel. On the second attempt he made contact. Arrangements were made to meet his client at the Riverwood condo.

Keel had a hearty laugh when he responded to Sage's page call and saw Dreadnought sitting in front of the condo. Sage had remodeled the classic Cadillac to accommodate his business requirements. Stainless steel racks ran from bumper to bumper to hold ladders and bars. The rear seat had been removed. A deck ran from the front seat to the rear window. Under the deck was a clear storage space that could be accessed from either the rear doors or the trunk.

"I bet you get the bird from a lot of Cadillac owners."

"Right," said Sage. "I just give them a big smile. Why should I ride in an old bucking truck when I can ride in style?"

"Pull forward through the garage door and pull a hard right into the space next to my Jeep. Here's a door opener to keep in your road monster."

On the way upstairs, Keel gave Sage all the keys and codes necessary to navigate around the building. In the unit, Keel said, "Dump your bag in the guest room," indicating the hall to the left. "Then join me in the kitchen. The sun's almost setting. It's time for a drink."

Keel was already pouring himself a Jim Beam when Sage arrived in the kitchen. He then added water from the spigot of a very large, bright orange container that looked extremely out of place in a well-appointed kitchen.

"This is one of the water coolers we keep for the roundup crews. I bring in spring water for drinks and ice cubes. I can't stand all the chlorine they use in town water."

"I have a wonderful deep well at my place," said Sage.

"Help yourself to anything that's there," said Keel as he declined to offer bartending services. "If you want something that's not there, leave a note on the counter or put the empty bottle there. I have a lady who comes in periodically to tidy up. She replenishes anything that's getting low."

Sage turned to a multiple-door closet. The outer double doors had a decorative hardwood design outside with shelves on the inside, as in a refrigerator door. Behind that were two more doors with shelves on both sides. The inside of the outer door was lined with bottles of booze and mixers. The inner shelves had non-perishable foodstuffs.

Sage selected a bottle of vermouth and Beefeaters to build his martini. Keel led the way to the balcony. One of the mechanical storm shutters had been lowered to protect the table from the glare of the setting sun.

The two men raised their glasses to one another and then took a sip.

Apparently Keel was never one to dance around a point. "Can't let you start that painting tomorrow."

Sage immediately came to a full alert. Was his commission in jeopardy?

Keel continued, "I've just been advised that a court order has been issued giving the Osceola Sheriff permission to search this condo. They were at the ranch this morning. I can't even go on my own property right now. They'll be here tomorrow morning. They aren't going to find anything, so I'm humoring them for the moment."

"This is part of the investigation into that grave site find on your property?"

"Yeah, I don't know a single thing about them, but the States Attorney keeps pressing the issue."

"Did they finish excavating the site?"

"It took a while, but eventually they uncovered 20 graves. Only one has been identified. The forensic people say that the victims are all young males. They got lucky on the oldest grave. There was a metal pin in the right leg, which was identified as belonging to a World War II vet who disappeared from this area in 1948. Since I'm the only one that's been around that long, they keep sniffing around here."

"If you didn't do it, then there must be someone else."

"That's where the rub comes in. Since the sheriff can't come up with anyone else, the SA keeps looking at me."

"It hasn't been that long since the bodies were found, so there's a lot of investigating yet to be done. Did the fire get to the ranch house?"

"No, it was on the other side of the lake and never got close."

"Good. I'd hate to have seen that wonderful old site destroyed."

As Keel had been talking and sipping his bourbon, Sage notice that Keel made frequent glances over Sage's shoulder. As Sage moved to find out what the attraction was, Keel said, "Don't turn around. I think we're being watched. Excuse me a moment."

Keel drained his glass, stood up and headed for the kitchen. Since Sage was facing the interior, he saw Keel come out into the shadowy entry hall with a large pair of binoculars, which he trained on the condo around the bend in the shoreline. He watched for a couple of minutes before disappearing back into the kitchen.

When Keel returned with his refill he said, "Go get another drink and while you're at it, take a look and tell me what you seen in the top corner condo across the way."

Sage made the trip to the hallway with the glasses. After an adjustment, he focused on the indicated unit. There was no patio furniture. The window verticals were closed except for a narrow opening behind the sliders. Sage focused his attention on that point. Slight motion greeted his prolonged scrutiny. He couldn't distinguish anything but a moving shape.

When Sage returned to the deck, Keel raised his eyebrows.

"Someone seems to be looking out a narrow opening," said Sage.

"That unit has been vacant for some time. If we'd wander over there, I'd bet we'd find an Osceola Sheriff or SA car in the parking lot."

"What are they up to?"

"Since those bodies were found on my land, they must be mine..... at least that's the thinking of the SA, so he's watching, hoping I'll slip up."

"What do they expect you to do? They tell you in advance they are going to search your place. Aren't they afraid you'd destroy any incriminating evidence?"

"I haven't the foggiest idea. I can't destroy anything, because I have nothing to destroy."

"Ummm," said Sage. "It would appear they are looking for something you can't burn in the fireplace or dump down the toilet. There's a garbage chute in this place, isn't there?"

"Come to think of it, they may have that covered too. The other day there was a guy thumping around in the dumpster. I assumed he was breaking up a clog in the chute. That happens occasionally."

"If they are expecting to catch you removing something, there would have to be someone watching your front entry too."

"You're probably right," said Keel with a smile. "Tonight, I think I will test your theory. Go get settled in your room. In half an hour I'll take you to dinner at the Surf."

When Sage heard Keel moving around the outside, he came out of his room. Keel was holding a cardboard box. Sage opened the outer door. Keel stepped through. "Will you lock up?"

Sage used his newly acquired keys to do as requested.

"You're right," said Keel. "There's someone on the roof of the West Wing, the condo on the other side of the retention pond. There's a fake owl on the corner to keep the pigeons away and a head is bobbing around behind it. At this hour there shouldn't be anyone there."

As Sage turned around he glanced in that direction. "You know, someone is going to have to find out what is in that box."

Keel smiled. "Right, and all they'll find is a bunch of used books. But someone is going to have to go through each one to make sure there aren't any nasty pictures hidden in them."

In the garage, Keel had Sage open the back of the Jeep so he could dump in the box. "I could put the box in my storage locker, but they'd probably tear it apart looking for it.

"I'm a great one for jerking chains," said Sage, "but there are times when it may not be in one's interest to do so. This sounds as if this might be one of those times. Of course, that box in the back end is just a rattle instead of a jerk."

"That's right. I'm just looking for a little information, such as how close are they watching me. It annoys the crap out of me to have to put up with all this foolishness."

"You know you didn't have anything to do with those graves, but so far they don't know that. They'll continue to harass you until they are convinced it was someone else."

"And in the end, I'll bet Burke won't even say he's sorry."

"Burke?"

"Yeah, the State Attorney."

Sage nodded to acknowledge the information.

When Keel pulled out of the garage, he was blocked from entering the street by an unmarked car. A plainclothes deputy stepped to the driver's window. "Mr. Keel, there's a court order to search you condo. Nothing can be removed prior to the execution of that order. We'll have to take that box you have in the rear. And who are you?" The deputy radiated ill will as he stared at Sage.

"This is Mr. Grayling, my artist. We're going out to dinner. Go ahead and take that box of books, but I want them back tomorrow so I can trade them in at the used bookstore. I need some fresh reading material."

The deputy glowered at Sage for a moment before retrieving the box from the back of the Jeep.

"Who was that sour bastard?" said Sage, as they pulled around the sheriff's car.

"Don't know. He's a new one. They all act as if they all have a stone stuck in their frog."

"What?"

"Got a rock stuck in their hoof."

Sage smiled as he caught up with the idea. He decided to change out of his Rockports into his cowboy boots so he could look down on little people. He'd have to be careful because Keel was only about 5'10".

Since Keel was so well known at the Surf, there were numerous greetings as they were led to a prime table, but Sage also noted a number of surreptitious glances as well as a couple of hostile glares. Keel also noted the various reactions.

"When this mess is straightened out, I'm going to have to have appropriate responses for certain of our 'better than thou' bluebloods and high-echelon snots."

"Oh, really?"

"Yeah, there are some around here that don't like sharing their exalted position with a cracker cowhunter. They don't realize they are the interlopers. I'm taking names and remembering faces."

When the waiter left, Sage became serious. "Mr. Keel...."

"Just Snapper. For a long time a first name and a handshake sealed bargains for huge herds of cattle and vast tracts of land."

"Okay, Snapper it is. I answer best to Sage. What I was getting at is that this investigation seems to be getting rather intense and it seems to be pointed in your direction. From the reactions I saw as we came in here, this story is slopping over into the community and it is or will be adversely affecting you. Do you have an attorney to look after your interests?"

"No. If I hire an attorney, that will be seen as an admission of guilt."

"A lot of ancillary damage can be done if there is no one to keep all the participants in line."

"I know, but that's not the answer. See that couple at the table over my left shoulder?"

After Sage glanced at the stern looking pair, Snapper said, "That retired colonel can't stand it that an old fart with cow manure on the toe of his boot could afford to use his fancy house for hay storage. That kind is more than willing to believe the worst. The only real defense is the truth."

"There are murder investigations going on all the time. Usually, the authorities are pretty tight-lipped under such circumstances. If the radio reports I heard as I was coming into town are any indication, there is a lot of explicit information floating around."

"Too much. The Osceola SA, David Burkes, is a young buck who

went through a savage battle with a law school competitor to win
his job. A successful conclusion to one of the biggest cases in the
state's history could insure his job in the coming election. Burke
is playing this case for all it's worth. He's giving too many press
conferences and each time a little more of the investigation slips
out."

"And, I take it, that you are the prime suspect."

"Yep," said Keel.

"And it appears that Mr. Burke is willing to tap the public
coffers rather heavily to put at least two surveillance teams on your
doorstep."

"He doesn't have any case other than the bodies were found on
my land and I'm the only one with a long enough tenure to have
added a body every couple/three years."

"You're not the only one on the ranch."

"Oh, I've had hundreds of ranch hands over the years, but if one
were to last ten years, he'd be considered a family treasure."

"How about the ownership of the ranches on that side of the
lake?"

"They've changed hands too many times. No one has sufficient
continuity. I've known all three owners. One is dead and the others
moved into the city the same as I did."

By the time they had finished a leisurely dinner and driven back
to the condo, the box of books had been placed along the wall in
front of the Jeep parking space.

Sage opened the back door so Snapper could put the box back
in the Jeep. "What do you want to bet that they are going to want to
search Dreadnought?"

"Dreadnought?"

"That's what I call my Caddy."

"Why do you think that?"

"Unless they have some sort of surveillance down here, they don't
know if that box you carried downstairs is the same as was in the

Jeep. What you took out of your place could be locked in my car."

Before turning on the lights in his unit, Snapper checked the neighboring condos. "Both lookouts are still manned as far as I can see. You're right. This investigation is really eating into his budget. They've sent samples from each body in for DNA profiles in their attempt to identify the bodies. I understand such testing isn't cheap."

"That's my understanding too. Are they checking your DNA?"

"So far, no. They probably don't have anything to compare it with. The unofficial word is that each body was completely naked and wrapped in a blanket."

"That doesn't help with the identification of the victim either."

"Right." Snapper took a tall glass from the cupboard, stoked it with ice and filled it with water. "I've had enough to drink, but help yourself. I'm going to watch the news and then turn in. I don't know when the authorities will be here to route us out in the morning. If we can get breakfast before they come, fine. If not, I'll buy at Denny's."

At 7:30 in the morning, the doorbell rang. Sage had heard Snapper thumping and bumping around much earlier. He'd lain in bed a while longer, but the guilt of letting an old man get the day started so much earlier than he, caused him to move his bones. He just finished in the bathroom when the authorities arrived. Sage was pulling on his boots when there was an over exuberant pounding on the door, which caused Sage to borrow one of Tinna's favorite words, *"Schieße!"* The thunderous knock was followed up by an equally obnoxious shout, "Out."

Sage felt the tingle in the hair along the back of his neck and knew he was about to do something that would not be in his best interest. He grabbed his Elph digital camera from his bag and quickly took a couple of pictures showing the layout of his room and the position of all his property. Then he took a seat at the writing desk sitting sideways so he faced the door. When the door slammed against the wall, the flash went off in the face of a bull of a man in civilian clothes.

"What are you doing?" bellowed the surly official.

"I want to know who will be plowing through my things."

"Smartass. Get out. We have a court order. Leave the premises."

The hulk had not entered the bedroom, so Sage could only get by him by stepping into the little hall that ran into the bath. As Sage side-stepped into the front entry, he nearly ran over a figure charging in the front door, who could best be described as a bantam rooster, complete with swagger and plumage. The swagger was interrupted when he almost ran his nose into the second button above Sage's belt buckle. To see the dapper little thing from his 6'6" advantage, Sage had to arch his neck as if he was inspecting a spot on his shirt.

At that moment, Keel appeared in the kitchen doorway. "Oh, Sage, I see you've run into our notorious state attorney, Davie Burkes."

"You're supposed to be out of here," growled Burke as he retreated from Sage's belly button. Turning to the lackey who had followed him in the door, he said, "Escort these two out and pick up the keys for the Jeep and that abortion parked next to it."

Sage scowled. "My car isn't part of your investigation."

"It is until I've determined that no evidence has been sequestered in it since you arrived."

Turning his attention back to the deputy as he stepped around Sage, he commanded in his less than authoritative voice, "When you pick up the computer, make sure you get all the storage devices."

Burke disappeared into the interior. The deputy held out his hand. When Sage hesitated, the officer said in a low voice, "I'd suggest handing over the keys. If you don't, he'll drag that car out and tow it to Kissimmee where he'll break in and tear it apart. Let me have the keys and I'll be careful."

Sage unhooked the keys from his ring and dropped them into the upturned palm. "I'm Sage Grayling."

"Mr. Grayling. I'm Arty Misconi. I'm a deputy state attorney from Osceola County and I like your wheels."

A piercing shriek came from the master bedroom area. "Misconi."

As the deputy headed in, Keel jerked his head toward the front door. With a big grin on his face Snapper said, "I think that little pip-squeak just found that there's no computer in there."

They caught the elevator before Burke could interfere with their breakfast escape. When Snapper stepped off the elevator he moved briskly into the garage, turning left instead of right. At the opposite end of the garage from the Jeep was a new Cadillac with gold trim and all the bells and whistles. Quickly they were out the door and headed for Denny's.

After the coffee arrived, Sage remarked, "I doubt if Norman Vincent Peal would have approved of our actions this morning."

"You're too young to have read that," said Snapper.

"It was required reading by a school counselor who didn't like my attitude. What happened to your computer?"

Keel tapped his temple with a forefinger. "The only computer I can use is right here. I'm too old to try figuring out all that new stuff. All that I need I can carry between my ears and Burke can't have that one. Why would he want my computer, if I had had one?"

"I understand that serial killers like to keep count or keep newspaper accounts of their exploits. He's probably hoping he'd come up with some incriminating information. Most people think they can delete items from their computer, but in most cases it is still there, but it's difficult to access unless you have the software and know how to use it."

"You know, you're too tall to be on Burke's guest list. In fact, I think it was hate at first sight."

"I got that impression too. Diminutive males always bother me. They tend to stand on others to make themselves look tall. Burke appears to be a prime example of that syndrome."

It wasn't until late afternoon that Keel and Sage were permitted back into the condo. Keel went in first. "Son-of-a-bitch," shouted Keel as he stepped into the living room. The place was a shambles, but the main source of Snapper's irritation was the holes that had been knocked in the new sheetrock that had been put up for Sage's painting. "Why the hell did he do that?"

"He'll say that he had to be sure you hadn't hidden something in the new wall, but it was probably done to take a jab at me. Sorry about that."

Snapper gave him a wry smile as he began to clean up.

"Leave that for a moment." Sage pulled his Elph out of his belt pouch and made a thorough photographic record of the entire condo.

Dreadnought's keys were on the dining room table. "I'm going down to check my car."

"While you're gone, I'll call the drywall man to get back over here."

Chapter   3

—ɯɯ—

It was going to take at least four days for the walls to be ready to prime. Then Sage could get down to work. His client's legal problems were going to cost him a week's time.

Snapper didn't want to be around for all the dust and noise, so he headed for the ranch, leaving Sage to fend for himself. That didn't bother the artist one bit since he was very self-sufficient.

Because of recent abundant demonstrations of his inadequacies in Spanish, Sage fished out the appropriate language CD, loaded it into his Walkman and headed to Ron Jon's for a new bathing suit and beach towel. Since he was comfortable with his own sexuality, he opted for a skimpy Speedo instead of the voluminous baggies that seemed designed to hide instead of delineate.

When Snapper had taken Sage to the Surf for dinner he mentioned that the beach, a block east, was a good place for people watching. That's where Sage headed after changing into his Speedo. The beach was only sparsely populated on a weekday morning. Retirees walked the surf line looking for shells. Mothers tried keeping track of hyperactive youngsters.

Sage spread his towel and began timing his sun exposure

Beach Shanty, a rustic little tavern across the ramp from an upscale watering hole.

Sage took a seat at an empty table in the gloom of the back corner. After the Florida sun roast, the air circulated by the Humphrey Bogart fans felt good on his damp skin. The icy cold Coors completed the pleasurable interlude.

As his eyes adjusted to the low-light conditions, he surveyed the other before-noon imbibers. A couple of ancient drunks were having their first glasses of beer of the day at the end of the bar. A couple of young lovers were at the window overlooking the beach, but the view was being wasted as they paid exclusive attention to one another.

In the opposite dark corner was a strange looking creature who was watching Sage with the same intensity as the young couple at the window were expending on each other. The piercing gaze was accentuated by the dark skin around the eyes as they peered out from beneath a ferocious mane of black hair.

The apparition unwound the correct number of limbs, which were extra thin and extra long to stand. He took a strangle-hold on his longneck beer bottle and made his way to Sage's table. In a velvety-smooth voice that belied his discordant appearance, he said, "I know you. You're Grayling, a dusty, grey-green fish. You're the trompe-l'oeil painter who did the Pit paintings."

Sage stood and without his boots, he had to look up into those strange eyes. *This is a tall one.* Sage stuck out his hand as he said, "How'd you know?"

"A friend downloaded your ebook and asked me if I was the model for the skull with the long hair. I'm always the butt of any available graveyard humor." As he shook hands, he said, "I'm called Golem."

"Golem?"

"Actually, the name is Gordon Lemry but I've been stuck with Golem since junior high. At first I hated it, but now it serves my purpose. I carve self-portraits of a sort."

Sage looked a little blank. Apparently, Golem was used to the reaction. He pulled a long, narrow stainless steel folder from his hip pocket, from which he extracted what looked more like a book mark than a business card. It showed a thin abstraction of a head covered with a great black tangle of matter forming a mass of hair.

The head was elevated far above the peak of a roof on a metal mast.

"Now I know what you mean. Please join me," said Sage, motioning toward a chair across from him.

Golem slowly folded his long limbs in a very mechanical manner to get down to the chair. He smiled at Sage's intense scrutiny.

"Now, if I was an artist of your caliber, I wouldn't have to be a walking billboard flogging my wares."

Sage frowned.

"Those paintings you did of the Pit are stupendous. Someday I hope to see the originals."

"Thanks. Actually they are rather impressionistic compared to my normal style."

"You're from New Mexico aren't you? What are you doing here in Cuckoo Beach?"

"I'm about to start a commission."

"Here? In Cocoa Beach?" said Golem with obvious enthusiasm.

"Yep," said Sage with a laugh. "Just a few blocks from here."

Turning very serious, the black eyes moved closer. "Is it someplace where I could periodically see how such a piece of work progresses?"

"It's in a private condo, but I think the owner wouldn't mind letting another artist watch its development."

Golem drew back. "You're too kind, but I would like to see how a painting like you do develops."

"Right now there's nothing to see until the drywall man replaces the walls that I was going to paint. They were destroyed yesterday."

"Oh, you're working for Snapper at the Riverwood."

"How'd you know? Do you know Snapper?"

"This is a small town and everyone knows what everyone else is doing. Everyone knows Burke was hassling Keel. Burke is in deep doodoo if that case is still hanging around unsolved in November. Since Burke and Keel are of different political parties, Keel couldn't even buy his way out with a political contribution without it smelling too fishy. I'm afraid your friend is in for a long period of harassment and maybe more."

"How do you know so much about a case in the next county?"

"Oh, I'm kind of like a pet rock. No one worries about talking around a senseless, inanimate object."

Sage didn't pursue any more of Golem's self-deprecation. He'd rather establish an amicable relationship with the guy, who despite his appearance, was proving to be one of the more interesting individuals Sage had encountered in a long time.

Holding up the business card, Sage said, "Tell me about these."

"These are called 'Golems'—after me. They're self-portraits. They may not be great art, but they pay for my beer....food, rent, whatever."

"And?"

"And, there's not much to tell."

"Yeah, you bet. How about materials, studio....little things like that?"

Golem gave Sage a baleful look. "There's not much to it. I carve them out of palm logs and blacken the eyes sockets with a propane torch. I make eyes by driving six inch spikes with stainless vanity washers. The hair is a hunk a synthetic bow fender off the tugboats in the port."

"That's an awful skinny description between two artists."

Golem cracked back, "It's awful skinny calling me an artist."

"You have a much more creative bent that most artists I know."

Long, narrow, sandaled feet shuffled uncomfortably under the table. "I can't really call myself an artist, like you. I've never gone to school. The closest thing to an artist I know is a couple of tiki carvers who live here."

"I never went to school either. I taught myself all I know, but I still consider myself an artist....more successful than a lot of art school grads I know."

Sage didn't want to frighten Golem off, so he said, "You come here often?"

"Yeah, this is kind of my office where people can find me."

"I've got to go now but I'll let you know when I start the painting. It will be three walls of a dining room." Sage stood up. "It's been a pleasure talking to you. Until next time." The pair shook hands.

Sage had the condo all to himself that night. Snapper had asked him to answer the phone and deal with any important calls. There was one call that needed attention. It was from a Detective Tony Lopez from the Osceola Sheriff's Office. He began by saying, "The SA was really ticked that you had another car there when he was searching your premises and you said nothing about it. He's sending me and a forensic tech over tomorrow to check that Cadillac."

Sage knew there was no phone at the ranch and that Snapper hated cell phones. Other than driving all the way out there in the dark along unfamiliar secondary roads, there was no way to pass the word along. In the liquor cabinet there was a key box. Sage found a set of keys for the Caddy. If the situation got out of hand, he could always come up with the keys.

At precisely 10:00 am the doorbell sounded. Lopez was standing there alone.

"Where's your tech?" said Sage as he answered the door.

"Left him and his equipment in the lobby. Where's Keel?"

"He's staying at the ranch until he gets done," indicating the drywall man, who was working on the damaged walls. "There's no way to reach him."

The deputy grimaced. "The SA said to bust a window if need be, but search the car."

"You don't really think there will be anything incriminating in a brand new car. The last grave is much older than the car."

"I know that and you know that, but the SA has other things in mind."

"Yeah, harassment," said Sage.

"I didn't say that."

"I found a set of Caddy keys. I'll go down with you and we'll see if they fit."

As the pair waited for the elevator, Sage said, "I was never long in math but according to my calculations you guys are looking for a collection of items less than 3 1/2 inches wide and that can be carried in a bread box. Since all the victims were young males, I suspect you are looking for a cock and balls trophy collection."

Lopez stuck a foot in front of the light so the elevator door wouldn't close. He looked up at Sage for a long moment. "I don't see anything wrong with your mathematical skills. Do they tell you anything else?"

"I've only been here a couple of day and I'm a stranger in these parts. Outside of some simple addition and subtraction, not much."

"Like what?"

"Well, you find 20 bodies on a bloke's ranch. According to the news reports a new body was added to your little cemetery every couple of years, starting in 1948. That would mean that if there is one murderer, he'd be getting pretty old. Of course, it could be a family affair being passed down from father to son or maybe from lover to lover."

"How'd you come up with the trophy item?"

"The murderer seems to have a fixation on guys. Hand, feet, ears wouldn't be distinctive enough. Heads would have been too large to fit on a 2x4 in a wall. If the trophy was ears, eyes, fingers, toes, you'd be checking even smaller containers."

"Ever think of a career in law enforcement? We could use some more mathematicians."

Sage laughed. "Then I might have to put up with the Burkes of the world."

Lopez started to agree but thought better of it. Instead he unblocked the door light and punched the first floor button.

There was only a cursory examination of the Cadillac. As Sage watched the tech go through the car, he asked Lopez, "How did Burke react to not finding a computer?"

"At first he thought that Keel had removed it. We finally convinced him that there was no hookup or sign of a computer ever being there."

"Why was he so interested in finding a computer?"

"A lot can be learned from both the current files and the deleted files, which our techs can recover. Also much can be told about what websites are visited. As an example, a pedophile can't seem to resist gong to pedophile sites while in the privacy of his home in the middle of the night. It's a good source of background info on anyone."

Sage went to the beach for a little more sun exposure. When he stopped in the Beach Shanty, the bartender told him that Golem had been there earlier, but someone had left word that a chunk of tugboat bow fender material had washed up on the beach in Cape Canaveral. He went to see if it was worth salvaging.

Sage had a beer before going back to the condo. The drywall man was wet sanding the compound he'd put on the day before. Even though there was no cloud of dust, Sage opted for the breezy humidity of the deck instead of the air conditioned interior. The condo where the watchers had been stationed now had closed verticals. When he'd absorbed as much Spanish as he could take for one day, Sage decided to find the used bookstore he'd noted on an earlier trip.

To exit through the door next to his parking space Sage had to cramp the wheels on Dreadnought, which produced a loud tire squalling, when it made a tight turn. That sound set his teeth on edge. Since the space directly behind him was vacant, Sage backed partially into it so he could make a leisurely left turn and go out the other door by the pool. As he approached the door, another tenant was entering the garage. The open door admitted strong mid-day light into the normally gloomy garage. As he passed Snapper's Cadillac, he noticed a swish of pink around the left rear tail light. The driver's side paralleled an interior wall. Sage pulled over. The incoming car passed, leaving the door up, figuring the exiting driver would close it. Sage stepped out of Dreadnought to inspect the pink smudge. As he sidled down along the Caddy he could see letters spray-painted all along the side. The crude letters spelled out "PERVERT."

Grinding his teeth at the wanton vandalism as well as the leap to judgment, Sage first scrutinized the floor to see if he was destroying anything of value. There was nothing that he could see.

Turning his attention to the letters, Sage could easily surmise that the perpetrator was no graffiti artist. Even teenybopper street gangs displayed greater skills with a spray can than this bastard. There were a lot of runs where he got too close. Parts faded as the can was pulled away. One distinctive move that he noted was that the can-wielder always made a slight hitch upward and to the right before making vertical strokes. He even did it on both sides of the letter "V."

Without going down the alley between the car and the wall, Sage took as good a set of pictures as possible with his Elph. He didn't want to be accused of destroying evidence.

Sage returned to the idling Dreadnought, pulled out of the garage and closed the door behind him. He sat for a bit deciding what to do. He didn't want to dial 911 because it wasn't an emergency. He didn't have the local police number, but the station was a block from the Surf.

There was a parking space right in front of the door. Inside the glass door was a tiny room with a couple of steel chairs. To the left was a button with a sign that said, "Push." Then there was a long, horizontal glass window obscured by a mini blind. On the end wall there was a mounted camera near the ceiling. Under it was a steel door with an electronic lock. On the right wall was a clear plastic pamphlet holder that sported an assortment of dead bugs.

Sage surveyed the public reception office of the Cocoa Beach Police, which had fewer amenities than the interrogation room he'd recently encountered in Portland, Oregon.

As he turned, a disembodied female voice said, "Help you?"

"No, you can't help me." Sage straightened to his full height and purposely strode back to Dreadnought. He'd have to let Snapper deal with that crew. He didn't feel inclined to be treated like a terrorist or some unclean creature. Before pulling away from the curb, he consulted his map so he could find his way to the ranch.

Even with all the bumps in the lane, Dreadnought glided down the rise to park beside the Jeep. He beeped the horn a couple of times to announce his arrival.

Snapper stepped into the doorway of a large building and yelled, "Back here."

When Sage made it to within conversational distance, Snapper said, "What brings you way out here?"

"Oh, a little problem came up that I thought you might want to consider. Step into the shade." Sage selected the image on his Elph showing the side of the Caddy. "From that view you can't read it all, but it says, 'PERVERT'."

"Bastard," said Snapper with more feeling than Sage had ever heard the old rancher use before.

"I spotted it as I was leaving the garage. Since I didn't have the police number, I drove to the station, but I didn't report it."

Snapper raised an eyebrow.

"Have you ever been in that station?"

"No."

"Don't go unless you want to be made to feel like a terrorist bent on eliminating the entire force. You're supposed to make your complaint to a mini-blind."

Snapper shook his head. "Wonder if this stuff will come off or if I'll have to have it painted."

"I have no idea. It depends on what kind of paint it is. The only thing I can tell you is that it is hot pink."

"Guess I better go back to town and take care of this mess."

"Do you think it could be someone from the condo?"

"Don't think so. Most are older folks and I've been on friendly terms with all those who live there. But, you never know when it comes to something like this. That garage is supposed to be locked. I wonder how he got in."

"That's no problem. There are bushes on either side of the door.

At night, just wait until a car comes out and duck around the corner. There's probably any number of other ways too."

"Oh, look at this," said Snapper. He stepped into the shed for a moment and came back with a bridle with a snaffle bit. "There was something wrong with the view through the farmhouse window. Remember the nail in the porch post?"

Sage nodded.

"This bridle used to hang on that nail." He handed the bridle to Sage, who hung it from his shoulder as they went back to lock the house.

Chapter 4

—ɯ—

When Snapper got back to the condo, he examined the additions to his Caddy's paint job with utter disgust. Anonymous acts were below contempt on his honor scale. He was a direct person with the guts to stand up for his convictions.

A call to the Cocoa Beach PD netted a female officer, who observed the damage before placing a call to another officer. She waited in her car until the second car pulled alongside. After a brief exchange, the first car left.

"Triage?" said Sage.

"Beats me."

The second officer had a camera and a finger print kit. It took half an hour before he announced that the vandal had left no physical evidence. He completed his report and departed.

Snapper shook his head and said, "I'll take it to a detail shop down south on A1A to see what they can do."

"The best evidence is the painting itself. Pull outside into the light and let me take a better picture. Then I'll follow you to the shop and bring you back. That work will take a while."

****

Finally, the time came to paint. The walls were primed. The cartoons were pounced onto the walls. The paint caddy was laid out and the lights were in position. Keel was planning on returning to the ranch to complete a project he'd started. Sage had asked if there would be any objections to letting Golem occasionally drop by to watch the progress of the painting. Snapper had seen Golem around and figured he was innocuous, so he had no reservations about letting the strange looking creature into his condo.

Sage didn't plan on starting the actual color application until the next morning. With Snapper gone, he was left to his own devices for the evening. He checked the amount of space in the freezer before heading to the grocery store for a supply of TV dinners that would be his main fare during much of the painting project.

With sort of a "last meal" attitude Sage ended up at Coconuts on the beach, where he enjoyed a rare New York strip surrounded by a couple of martinis. As the place started its loud transition from dining to entertainment, Sage fled the ever increasing decibels.

As he headed for Dreadnought, he spotted a step van that could only be Golem's judging by the sculptural images painted all over it.

Sage reversed directions, and found Golem at the corner of the bar in the Beach Shanty where he could stretch his long legs. The dark, grim eye sockets were moderated by a broad, compressed lip smile that showed no teeth.

"Hi, Golem, I figured that had to be your van outside."

"How could you have possibly guessed?" came a silky, smooth reply followed by a chuckle. "I hear you have a rather distinctive vehicle yourself. I also hear that your boss's Caddy also has, shall we say, a mark of distinction."

"Word certainly gets around," said Sage as he settled on a stool and motioned to the bartender for a beer.

"This is a little town made up of a lot of older folks who have the time to tend the business of others. Don't get me wrong, those are also the people that can stroke their whims and buy my golems."

Sage took a pull from the recently arrived longneck before

asking, "Are you still interested in following the development of my painting?"

The loose-jointed form on the barstool suddenly straightened. "You bet."

"In the morning, I'll begin applying color. Unless some disaster occurs, I'll keep my nose in the paint until I'm done. When I'm working, I'm a lousy host after about five minutes."

"Anything you say."

"If you like, drop by tomorrow morning and I'll buzz you in. I'll give you a cup of coffee, but in a few minutes I'll fade into the painting. You can watch and then let yourself out when you're ready."

"Is Snapper there?"

"Not right now, but he'll be coming and going. Under the circumstances, he'd rather be out on the ranch with no phone and almost impossible to find. There's an ever-rising clamor over those bodies. News hounds want to use him as the source of their Pulitzer. Others consider themselves shrewd enough that, given the chance, they can wrangle some admission out of him that will give them their fifteen minutes of fame."

"Ha, that will be the day when some rube can get anything out of Snapper. He's one tough old man. I understand he has a hell of a history. If this ever goes to trial, the prosecution will have a field-day. It's only been in the last few years that civilization took hold in these parts."

"You're saying that Snapper had a colorful life that could come back to haunt him?"

"Right now it's just quaint folklore, but that sneaky little prick, Burke, will use anything to bring a big man down."

"Have you heard anything on how his case is coming?"

"They've got five or six of the bodies tentatively identified. Those are the latest because communications and records keeping have become so much better. Probably some of the early ones will never be identified."

Sage passed on the offer of another beer. "I'm two martinis ahead and I have to be ready to go in the morning."

When the travel alarm went off at 6:00 am, Sage rolled out of bed with his game face on. Even though he had no plans of going anywhere, he passed through the shower and shaved. He had set up Snapper's automatic coffee pot the night before so he could pour himself a cup while preparing breakfast.

Sage's whole morning procedure was a formulaic freeing of his mind from outside considerations. Once he stepped in front of his painting, he focused on translating his mental images onto the surface. However, once the decisions had been made on how to proceed, Sage's mind had a tendency to concoct other creative projects. To reduce frustrations, he sopped up excessive mental activity by plugging his Walkman into his ear. It was loaded with the current language of interest.

The interior walls of the ranch house had never been painted. Somewhere along the line varnish had been added. The surface had turned golden yellow, which was further enhanced by Snapper's afternoon sun. Sage squeezed large amounts of the various yellow pigments onto his palette to begin laying in the background. It was busywork, so the Spanish lesson began early.

At 10:00 Golem called and Sage buzzed him in. Since this was the first visit, Sage stepped out to hail him, but the sculptor demonstrated that he already knew the way by turning right as he came out of the elevator. His eyes swung in the right direction. Sage wondered how his guest always seemed to be a step ahead of everything.

"You look different this morning," said Sage.

"I left off the eye shadow. I'm not flogging my wares this morning."

"Are you a coffee drinker?"

"You bet."

Sage led the way into the kitchen, pointing to the mug tree and the coffee pot. "Sugar and sweetener is in the canister and if you haven't been weaned, there's a powdered creamer in the fridge."

Golem was content with black coffee. Sage headed down the hall to the dining room.

"Oh, wow," said Golem as his eyes traveled over the cartoon and the area where Sage had been laying in the background with a three-inch brush. "I can't conceive of even starting on a project of this size and complexity. It takes me only an hour or two to carve one of my pieces."

Sage laughed. "I hate selling. The longer I can drag out the painting part, the less marketing I have to do."

"I'd like to expand my horizons so I don't have to be a walking billboard all the time."

"You'll figure out something." Sage nodded toward the dining room table and chairs, which had been moved down the one step into the living room. "Park yourself. I'm going back to work. When you get tired, just walk out." Sage picked up his brush and turned on his Walkman.

A couple of hours later Sage took a break. Golem was gone and his cup was in the sink. Sage settled for a bowl of ramen noodles before returning to his painting.

At 5:00 o'clock Sage took a martini break on the deck. He was interrupted by the phone. Since Snapper wasn't particularly taken with modern gadgetry, he didn't have an answering machine so Sage could monitor the incoming calls. Sage wasn't expecting any calls and Snapper hadn't renewed his request to take calls, so he ignored the whole thing.

Before returning to work, he tossed a TV dinner into the microwave. After eating, he washed his utensils and took the garbage out to the chute by the elevator. The chute door was being stubborn. He tried turning the handle in the opposite direction.

"You have to jerk it," came a scratchy comment from somewhere near his right elbow. Sage jumped. "They should fix that thing. Sometimes I can hardly get it open."

Hovering in close proximity to his right hip was a mere wisp of an ancient woman. At least she looked old because of her emaciated condition and her crepe skin. She was dressed in a short, sleeveless shift with a scoop neck. Even though it was a good wrap for the existing weather, it seemed a poor fashion choice for the tiny woman.

Sage was certain she hadn't been on the walkway when he came out of Snapper's condo. He looked around to find where she had been. The screen door to the first condo on the east wing was open.

"You're Sage Grayling, the painter," said the woman with authority.

"That's what they tell me when I'm having a good day."

"That's a good one," cackled the old gal. "I'm Mona Hatfield. I'm the condo spy, if you ask the other residents of this pile of rocks. I'm not really spying on you. It's just that I am observant and my condo has the best view in this place. Besides the front and back view, I have side windows that overlook the patio, elevator and all the west building walkways. Whenever something moves, I'm attracted."

"Well Mona, I don't plan on doing anything worth watching," said Sage as he dropped the sack down the chute.

"It's more fun watching the guys who are watching you."

"Oh, really?" said Sage as he perked up." Watching me?"

"Well. Watching Snapper's condo, but he's not here and they're setting up again."

"Where?"

"In the condo behind your unit....in the top floor, vacant unit."

"How do you know?"

"I walk every morning and evening. I don't like walking on sidewalks so I go cross-country between these three condos and the church parking lot. The county cars are back." His informant smiled benignly.

"Thanks for the warning. I'll be sure to close the drapes if I'm not properly dressed. Oh, did you know they use the roof behind your unit?"

"Oh, really?"

"Yeah, watch the fake owl."

"Oh, my." Mona silently skittered back toward her condo.

Instead of going back to his painting, Sage made a fresh pot of coffee and took a mug out to the deck where he watched the opening in the verticals in the next condo. Because it was dark inside, he couldn't see any activity. To be contrary, Sage lowered the hurricane shutters, blocking any view of the living room. With a smile he went back to his painting.

In the morning, Sage was back to his painting after his hygiene routine and breakfast. The phone had been ringing constantly. People were asking for Snapper. For the first few calls, Sage tried to explain that Snapper wasn't there. After a few smart comments, Sage simply listened only long enough to find out if Golem was calling and then hung up.

At 10:00 there was a discrete knock at the door. When Sage peered out the peep-hole he found Golem smiling back at him. When Sage opened the door he got a better look at Golem's crooked smile. "Figured you were tired of answering the phone, so I let myself in."

"How'd you manage that?"

"Being tall has its advantages. I can look over shoulders as someone is punching in the secret code."

Golem followed Sage to the coffee pot, as the phone rang again. "What's going on with that bloody phone?"

"You haven't been watching TV."

"No. What's happened?"

"Our dear Osceola County State Attorney just held a press conference. The election is coming and he needs to show progress on his mass murder case. He announced that he was declaring Snapper Keel to be a 'person of interest' and that Keel would be officially notified, if he could be found. That little scheming rodent is making it sound as if Snapper is in hiding.

"Snapper's at his ranch," said Sage. "I guess Burke can get away with saying that since there is no phone or electricity out there."

The two men took their coffee into the dining room as the phone rang again. Sage looked at his painting for a bit before he sighed and started cleaning brushes. "Do you want to take a ride? With that phone I'll soon be climbing the wall. I'd better drive out to the ranch and tell Snapper about this last sneak attack. It may be time for him to get a lawyer."

"Sure, I'll go with you. I'd like to see that old place. It's one of the local legendary, historical sites."

"How so?" said Sage as he settled the cover over the paints on his palette.

"It's the oldest single family ranch left. Most of the big chunks of land have been split up. Each of the Keels expanded their holdings. Snapper really added a lot of acreage."

The phone was ringing again. Someone was at the front door. "Let's get out of here," said Sage. He led the way to Dreadnought. Instead of exiting near the front door, he went out the east door. As soon as he was sure no one was in the path, he tickled Dreadnought, which leapt beyond hailing distance of anyone lurking about the front entry. He swung left to head for Highway 520. As he passed the next condo, where the surveillance team had been set up, Sage glimpsed a couple of men racing for a car. He kept an eye on the rear view mirror. The car came screaming past the big pond toward the street.

"Damn," said Sage. "I think we've picked up a tail."

"Turn right," snapped Golem. "Punch it. If the light is red go right. If green, go through."

Just as Sage made a California stop at the red light, the suspect car also made a right turn two blocks behind to follow Dreadnought.

As Sage headed south on A1A, Golem commanded, "Right into the church parking lot. Turn behind the building and slowly cross the street into the town houses. The street loops to the left and comes back to about half a block from where we started. Turn right and you'll be on your way." Golem smiled benignly as he settled back into Dreadnought's fine seat.

"Why would anyone want to follow me?" said Sage.

"Probably wants you to lead them to Snapper."

"It's no secret that Snapper is at the ranch."

"You know that really doesn't tell anyone much," said Golem with his crooked smile. "That's kind-a-like telling someone he's hanging out in Miami. It would be a heck of a lot safer hunting for Snapper in the city than it would be on the ranch, especially if Snapper doesn't want to be found."

"I think you're building a spook. When his Caddy was spray painted, I drove out to the ranch and told him of the vandalism and there was no problem."

"Yes, but he took you out earlier and you knew where to go. There aren't many people that know that and I'll bet you have a very good visual memory."

"Well. I'll grant it took a little effort to remember which of those trails to take."

"And you found him because he recognized you and wanted to be found."

"You know you're building a rather negative image of my boss. The Snapper I met is an easygoing, considerate individual, who seems to have everything working for him. From what I have seen and from what I feel by being around him, I see nothing to indicate he'd be inclined to kill all those boys.....young men."

"Don't get me wrong," said Golem. "I wasn't expressing my own opinion. Those would be the considerations of Burke and his crew. They're city boys and would be loath to step off concrete or blacktop. And I hear they have been chasing all the old stories concerning Snapper, which would quickly weaken their kidneys." Golem chuckled at his own image.

"This is the second time you've referred to Snapper's colorful past. What kind of color are we talking about?"

"You know how rumors and legends are built. It's rather common bar room talk that rustling was a major business hazard in Florida for decades except on the Circle K. Rustlers usually steered clear of Keel's ranch, but if someone got lost or stupid, that was the last mistake he made."

Sage remained silent for a bit while he searched the landscape for recognizable landmarks. "Is Burke trying to say that hanging rustlers and killing young men for some sort of weird gratification is the same?"

"He's probably trying to show that both are intentional killings.

There are apparently others besides rustlers. Of course, all that was before there was any law in these parts."

Sage noted that despite his loose-jointed, casual conversational presentation, Golem was intently memorizing the entire route. After a slow process down a rutted road, Sage pulled up to an opening in the fence that was protected by a cattle guard. "Everything you can see to the front is part of Snapper's spread."

Most of the land was as flat as a tortilla, with clumps of trees periodically breaking the skyline. Stands of trees surrounded small lakes.

After a considerable drive over a rough track, Sage eased over a small rise and tooted his horn. He spotted the black Jeep, but no Snapper. The lock was not on the front door, but no one came out.

"Maybe he's out on a horse," said Sage.

"He probably won't show himself until he knows who's with you. Let's get out and stand by the car," said Golem as he stepped out and leaned against the strut that held up the top rack.

Sage followed suit. A couple of minutes later Snapper sauntered around the old bunk house and joined the new arrivals.

"Hi Sage. You're Golem, aren't you?"

"That's me. How'd you recognize me without my makeup?"

"Oh, there are a few other hints. What brings you guys way out here?"

"I wondered why the phone started ringing incessantly," said Sage. "Everyone's looking for you. When Golem dropped by, he said Burke had given another press conference where you were the subject of discussion. Tell Snapper what your dear SA had to say."

"He didn't have much to say but used the opportunity 'not' to say things. He reported that he was going to officially notify you that you were a 'person of interest' in the mass grave case....if you could be found. He was giving the distinct impression you were in hiding. The reporters jumped on the announcement asking if Burke was seeking a warrant, any DNA evidence, witnesses and so forth. Burke would just smile knowingly and say, 'no comment'. He seemed to be padding his own popularity at your expense."

Snapper took on a look of sadness and shook his head before saying, "That's too bad, but I guess I'll have to do something."

"Golem tells me that Burke is collecting all the reports of your earlier exploits," said Sage. "I'll bet it isn't being done for a literary purpose."

Snapper snorted. "That's all old folk-lore. You know how things get exaggerated around cow-camp cooking fires."

"Don't discount how low that worm can crawl," said Golem. "He may not be able to get it into the court record, but he's good at influencing people with innuendos."

"You're probably right. I'd better go see Hack Gibbons. He's an old lawyer friend of mine."

Golem offered a crooked smile, but no comment.

Sage flipped his cell phone open. "I thought those were cell phone towers I saw on the way out. I'm getting a strong signal. You may not like phones, but how about getting a cell phone at least for the duration of this problem? That way I won't lose a day's work each time something comes up. If you don't want to receive calls, don't give out the number....except to me, of course."

Snapper grimaced. "I'll think about it."

"In any case," said Sage, "if it's all right with you I'm going to buy an answering machine so I can monitor the calls without going to the phone all the time."

"Do whatever you want. There's another phone jack in one of the shelves behind the poker table. It's closer than the rest. I guess I'd better head for Kissimmee if I want to catch Hack before it's too late. "Thanks, Golem, for passing along the information."

"While we're here, do you mind if I show Golem around? He's been following the progress of the painting."

"Go ahead. Just lock the door when you leave." Snapper spun around to head for his Jeep. Instead of turning back to the road where Sage had come in, Snapper took off cross country.

For the next hour Sage and Golem poked their noses into the

various buildings, walked around the acres of corrals and ended up on the dock, enjoying the breeze that ruffled their hair as well as the reeds along the bank. Sage took the opportunity to snap some marvelous bits of life for future paintings.

Golem reflected back on his tour. "Man-o-man, all of that beautiful vacant space. Most of the year I work under a tree somewhere. When it rains, I have to clear some space in my van if I absolutely have to work. Usually, I can out-wait the rain....that is called procrastination."

"I have a passing acquaintance with that term too."

"What kind of studio space do you have?"

"My primary painting studio is 20x100x18 feet high."

Golem didn't even answer. He just gave Sage the most baleful, mime look Sage had ever seen.

The trip home was a pleasant interlude of conversation on art conducted by Sage and local history and geography presented by Golem. Sage's background led him to notice etched glass doors on an old farmhouse or the fancy carved fascias. Golem took note of *Junkus Effucious* taking over a spongy pasture or the osprey nest on a power pole.

Before going home, Sage made a detour to a Walmart for an answering machine. At the condo he turned off the rings on all the phones but one, which he turned down to its lowest setting.

Snapper came home just in time to rescue Sage from a frozen dinner. "I'll buy you a shrimp dinner if you'll show me how to use one of these infernal things." Snapper held up a new cell phone.

"It's a deal."

The next morning Sage passed up a breakfast invitation to get an early start on his painting.

"Don't forget the bridle on the porch," said Snapper.

"I haven't, but I have to put in the nail first."

"The spots on that chair blanket are a brighter red."

"Okay. How about the color of the enamel on the tin bread box?"

"Don't remember. We've had several. Make it blue. That's the one I liked best."

The phone tinkled safely in the distance. The answering machine was set to pick up on the first ring. The call was from an Orlando Sentinel reporter asking for a call back.

"I'd better get out of here," said Snapper as he headed for the door. 'Got some shoppin' to do."

Sage had the day to himself. Golem didn't show up. The phone wasn't a constant irritation. Sage got in some good strokes.

After working through lunch, Sage was giving some consideration to dinner, when Snapper came through the door growling. "Mona Hatfield tells me the spies are back."

"Do you suppose they want to serve you with 'a person of interest' letter?"

"Hack says that Burke probably doesn't want to serve it....just beat me with it. Anyway I don't care if they do or not. What I came by for is to see if you'd help me this evening. I have some stuff in the Jeep to go out to the ranch. It's too heavy for me to handle alone. I'll buy you one of the best steaks in this part of the country over in Cocoa."

"How can I pass up an offer like that? Are you coming back tonight or should I drive over?"

"Oh, I'll bring you back."

Sage secured his pallet and changed into his cowboy boots before indicating he was ready.

Snapper hadn't identified the cargo. When the dome light came on, Sage couldn't help it—he laughed.

"Okay, have your fun," said Snapper. "I must be getting soft in my old age. After buying this place I've gotten addicted to a microwave. Old time cookin' just takes too long and it heats up the place."

"And a TV?"

"Hack told me I'd better keep up with what's going on in Kissimmee. Burke is playing dirty."

"How about a TV signal?"

"Tomorrow afternoon some guys are going to install a satellite dish."

Sage thumped the biggest box.

"A generator."

"I thought you didn't want to listen to one."

"That's my burden for having all this modern crap. And a cell phone to boot."

"It won't be long until you're into computers."

"Not until I'm shed of Burke. He'd keep taking them to see if I'm watching any porn."

They picked up a tail when they pulled out onto the street, but no one tried to serve any papers....even when they stopped for steaks.

Snapper offered the opinion that the guys were out of their jurisdiction. "They'll wait until I cross the county line."

Snapper had been right about the steaks. Sage's was absolutely perfect. The decor of Jake's Steakhouse was recent attic or vintage garage sale, which had initially caused Sage to question Snapper's tastes, but a friendly, homegrown service and the quality and quantity of the food had quickly converted him into a believer.

As the pair relaxed over an after-dinner coffee, there was a slight change in the background noise, which attracted both Sage's and Snapper's attention. A very broad figure filled the doorway. Jake had arrived. Everyone immediately became aware of his presence. Jake wore a broad smile. His eyes swept the room. When his gaze found a familiar face, Jake made a pistol pointing finger motion in its direction. When he found Snapper, the old cowhunter rated a double barrel finger salute. The gaze continued to sweep the room, but the double barrel salute had set wheels into motion. Two waiters were already hefting a broad, study bench toward Snapper's table. Another waiter was readying an oversized mug of black coffee to follow him to the designated table.

Jake, in a rolling walk, passed through the tables greeting patrons....even those he didn't know, until he reached Snapper, motioning him to remain seated. He extended his hand and began to sit as his bench was being slid under him.

"Old friend. You have been too long gone."

"You know the reason. I've been keeping my head down. This is my friend, Sage Grayling. He's reproducing my old ranch house in the condo dining room."

"Jake smiled as he gave Sage a firm, manly handshake. "You better get it right, young man. I'll spot any mistakes."

"He will, too," said Snapper with a laugh. "He's spent enough time contemplating his surroundings over a glass of shine."

Sage didn't smile soon enough, so Snapper supplied, "moonshine."

"Is Burke still on your back trail?"

"Yep. There's probably a carload of his minions in your parking lot right now."

"Oh really?" Jake stuck a thick finger into the air. He was immediately attended by a young waiter. "Take a smoke break in the parking lot. There should be an official car out there. Have a look and then tell me about it."

The two old friends verbally sparred with one another until the waiter returned. "There's an unmarked Chevy backed into a space just like the cops do. Two guys in suits are sitting inside with the A/C on."

Jake smiled broadly. "Give me five minutes' notice before you leave." Jake stood. The bench disappeared and Jake set sail for the kitchen.

"What's Jake going to do?"

"I don't know, but he'll think of something."

When they finished their coffee, Snapper attracted a waiter's attention and pointed to the door. Five minutes later, Snapper stood and dropped an obscenely large tip on the table and headed for the door.

Darkness had fallen while they had been inside. A large refrigerator truck was blocking the right hand entry and several parked cars. The hood was up and the driver was contemplating the motor compartment.

Snapper marched to his Jeep with Sage following. Moments later, the Jeep left by the other exit without a tail.

"Neat," said Sage. "How come that huge tip or was that to cover the bill?"

"Jake's never presented me with a bill since he opened. I grubstaked him decades ago. He paid back every cent. He considers my food to be his interest payment. Since I can't pay for anything, I help out the staff. Whoever's on duty that night will split the money."

They still didn't have a tail when they pulled into the secondary road. "I doubt if those guys will wander around here at night. We'll put the generator in the shed and the rest in the house. Then we'll head back for Cocoa Beach. The guys won't wait around. We could be staying the night or we could go out another way."

Sage was trying to keep track of their route at night. His visual references had changed. He was pleased that he had spotted the ranch entrance ahead of Snapper's turn.

"Better slow down or you're going to have that TV in your lap," said Sage as he shoved the bouncing carton back on top of the generator.

"Should have tied them down," said Snapper as he slowed to go on a bridge over a drainage creek.

WHAM...Carumph!

A blast of excruciating pain racked Sage's head and body an instant before he lost consciousness.

Awareness plucked at Sage's mind any number of times but he preferred to flee back into oblivion. Finally, he grabbed onto a strand of consciousness long enough to decide he must tolerate the pain long enough to find out what needed doing.

Suddenly, panic gripped him. He was in total darkness and he was hanging upside-down? He tried to investigate his surroundings. His right arm hurt badly and it wouldn't do his bidding.

With his left hand he felt around and finally came to the

conclusion he was being held by a seat belt. As his hand began to identify objects, memory started to return. He extended his search downward and touched Snapper and water.

It took three attempts before he could frame the word, "Snapper." No answer. He pinched the body and got no reaction.

Sage became aware part of the pain in his head was coming from his ears. He rapped on a solid object within reach and couldn't hear a thing above the incessant ring in his head. He uttered some words but heard nothing.

Sage's brain began to sluggishly function. He was hanging by a seat belt. Snapper was below him so the Jeep must be on its left side....in water. Feeling around, he found Snapper's head that was in the water. Using a handful of hair, Sage was able to shift his face to a position higher than the water.

Turning his attention to his own predicament, he found that his right arm ached miserably and his hand wouldn't work properly. Tender examination revealed a broken forearm.

His legs were numb. He had to get out of that seat belt, but when the buckle was released, he'd fall on Snapper. With great effort, Sage changed his position until he could bridge between the seat and the dash before he released the buckle. He fell hard on the armrest, but he avoided dropping his full weight on the unconscious rancher.

After maneuvering into a sitting position, Sage had to rest. Every movement seemed to be a major effort. While resting, he tucked his right hand into his shirt to keep it from painfully flopping around.

While his head cleared a little more, Sage tried to open the passenger door. It wouldn't budge. Carefully, he explored the surface. The door was wrinkled. The window glass was shattered but the core was still in place.

Sage's mental proclivities to arrange his world in logical order were returning. He had to get out of that steel box and find some help. Sweat was dripping off his chin. As he turned back to check the windshield, he felt a faint cooling on his cheek coming from the rear.

Slowly and painfully he worked his way over the generator crate.

The rear door was missing. Eventually, Sage found himself lying on spongy ground. The stars were shining brightly as he stared up. He worked his way into a sitting position. As he scanned the horizon, there wasn't a light in sight. Then a distant red eye winked at him. It took Sage a moment to realize the significance....a microwave tower. Cell phone. He groped around under his throbbing right arm. His cell phone was still on his belt.

The left hand was shaking so violently he had to lay the phone on his left thigh to see glowing, blue numbers. There was a good signal, but the charge was low. He carefully punched in 911. Before pressing the send button, he tried his voice. He was saying the words but he could hear nothing but the roar in his head. Another realization halted the placing of the call. Who would find them out there? He didn't know how badly Snapper was hurt. Also how long could an old man lie in even warm Florida water before hypothermia sets in? He didn't need an ambulance driver wandering around the wilds of Osceola County.

There was Snapper's daughter-in-law and grandson. They knew the way to the old ranch, but he didn't have a number or know how they were listed. Since he couldn't hear he'd probably be wasting the little time he had left on his battery.

The vision of Golem's old step van passed through his mind with all the depicted sculptures and his phone number.

Sage punched in that numbers and when the screen indicated the number had been dialed Sage waited a bit before he started talking. "Golem, this is Sage. I can't hear anything. Snapper's truck was blown up just before the ranch house. We need an ambulance." Sage repeated the message two more time in case it took Golem a while to get to the phone. If he wasn't home, he had an answering machine.

He broke the connection to call 911. At least he was pretty sure someone would answer. He didn't know where his call would go and he couldn't hear any questions so he gave the facts as concisely as possible. "Need an ambulance. There are two of us. Our car was blown up. I am deaf. We were blown off a bridge near the old Snapper Keel ranch house on the Circle K ranch." He gave the road designations as he knew them. "Keel is unconscious and in water. Snapper's grandson and daughter-in-law know how to get here. So does Golem, in Cocoa Beach." Sage gave Golem's number. "Send ambulance."

Sage snapped the phone back on his belt before hauling himself upright. He had to help Snapper. He shoved the TV and microwave boxes out onto the ground. There was no way he'd be able to shift the generator. With all the exertion, he was having trouble breathing. He called to Snapper, but he couldn't hear his own words.

When he wriggled his way back to the driving compartment, he briefly used the glow of the cell phone dial to get a look at Snapper's situation. His head was out of the water, but the major portion of the body was either under water or wet. Sage settled further into the space so he could check for a pulse. There was a weak one.

Since he couldn't find any blood, Snapper's injuries must be concussion type from the explosion. He could have internal injuries. Sage didn't want to wrestle him around, but he could feel the old man's body temperature had fallen. If Sage could manage it, there was enough room on the inclined plane of the driver's door that he could get Snapper's torso out of the water. He didn't want to aggravate any internal injuries, but it wouldn't matter if he died of hypothermia first. This could be a long wait.

With a supreme one-armed effort, Sage raised Snapper further out of the water. The exertion drained the painter's reserve. He crawled onto the generator case and passed out.

Sometime later he roused, but his whole body rebelled at the mere thought of movement. He was aware that the mosquitoes had found him. Swatting at them would extract an extremely high payment. If help hadn't arrived by first light, he'd have to try to walk out.

Later, Sage roused again. He had a pounding headache and the roar in his ears had not abated. However, another element had been added to his misery. It was a pulsating vibration that sent tiny pain signals to various spots in his body. Suddenly a brilliant light seared his fully dilated pupils....a helicopter.

Before Sage could get his body functional enough to crawl off the crate, Golem's lopsided grin appeared before him. The mouth was working, but Sage still couldn't hear the words.

Golem patted him on the shoulder and pointed in Snapper's direction. Sage could feel vibrations running through the vehicle. He lost track of time. At one point he was lifted out of the Jeep and placed on a stretcher. He remembered snippets of a helicopter ride, hospital scenes. His next fully conscious episode was to find himself in a hospital bed with a navy blue cast on his right forearm. His whole body mildly protested any movement even though Sage suspected he had been given a pain killer.

The metallic snick of the latch drew his attention to the door.

A nurse came bustling in. "Oh, good, you're awake. I'd better catch the breakfast cart before it disappears." The nurse pulled a U-turn and disappeared.

Sage was gratified to hear the nurse's comments even though they sounded like a poor, radio station full of static.

As Sage was testing his voice and hearing with "eny, meany, miney, mo," the nurse popped back into the room carrying a tray. Satisfied he could make himself understood, he said, "How's my friend Snapper Keel?"

"Oh, he's down the hall complaining about the foul taste of the water we use to make coffee."

"He must be feeling all right. Can I see him?"

"Not yet. Both of you had your innards jiggled around. The doctors want to run some more tests to make sure everything is working before you go bouncing around. Besides, there are a bunch of people who want to talk to you. Osceola deputy sheriffs are en route."

While Sage picked at his breakfast, he spotted the phone on the shelf along with the TV remote. After a detour through information, he had Snapper on the line.

"How are you feeling?" asked Sage.

"Ah, I'm all right. The fool doctors won't let me out of bed until they poke and prod some. You're the one that got broke up. That's your painting arm, isn't it?"

"Yeah, It'll be a while before I can handle a brush."

"Don't worry about it. Just leave your stuff where it is until you can get back to work."

"Thanks. Do you know what happened?"

"I hear you probably know more about it that me. There was an explosion and the next thing I know, I'm in an emergency room. You must have gotten help. How'd you do that?"

Sage told his boss what little he knew of the event, adding that without Golem they may still have been lying in the creek.

Their conversation was interrupted on both ends. Doctors arrived to conduct more tests on Snapper and a pair of Osceola deputies arrived to talk with Sage.

"Mr. Grayling, remember me, Detective Antonio Lopez? This is Deputy Vern Taylor. We're looking into your accident last night."

"What accident? What makes you think it was an accident? Somebody tried to kill us," said Sage with some heat. The concept that the explosion could be some sort of accident chased a lot of cobwebs out of Sage's mind.

"We don't know that yet," said Lopez defensively.

"It's a lot better assumption that someone planted an explosive device along the road which is normally traveled by only one person than it is to assume that somehow nature assembled the proper elements necessary to produce an accidental explosion that can send a new Jeep airborne."

Lopez threw his hand up. "Okay, okay. That was just a neutral opening remark. I wasn't trying to express any pre-judgments."

Sage tried moving into a more comfortable position on too short a bed. "Sorry, I'm not at my usual, sunny best. Can you tell me what you found? It was pitch black and I kept phasing out."

Lopez countered. 'First tell us what you remember and then I'll tell you about the scene. I'm going to record this interview." The detective pulled a tiny digital recorder from his pocket and placed it on the breakfast stand.

The deputy recited the introduction litany giving when and where, who was present and the purpose of the interview. With proper prompting Sage recited what little he knew and what he did.

Lopez asked a few questions, but it was obvious that Sage couldn't contribute much. The deputy concluded the recording.

"Your turn," said Sage.

"We didn't get there until after the helicopter took you two away. We had to find Keel's grandson and get him to lead us in. Just before you get to that rise where the house is located, there is a little bridge over a drainage canal. The bridge is made of a couple of pine logs spanning the creek and 2x8 planks covering. It appears that an explosive charge was placed under the far left corner as you approached. We found a trigger mechanism that set it off when the front left tire made contact. It took out the left log and most of the 2x8s. It lifted your Jeep about twenty feet. It must have flipped you about three-quarters of a revolution. You landed on the driver's side."

Sage was visualizing the scene and he didn't immediately respond.

Lopez continued on. "The initial inspection indicates that ammonium nitrate was used. The same stuff as in Oklahoma City. You're lucky it wasn't something else. This stuff has a powerful push but not the impact of other explosives. You guys were lucky you didn't get hit by the debris."

"Did you find any writing?"

"Why do you ask?" said Lopez.

"Someone spray painted Snapper's new Caddy the other day."

"Go get the laptop," said Lopez to Taylor.

After Taylor left the room Lopez said, "We found bits and pieces of what looks like a script painted on the bridge planks."

"I don't remember seeing anything there and Snapper never made any comment."

"There may be a reason. Sand was embedded in the paint. It looked as if someone had painted a message and then covered it with sand before it was dry."

"What did it say?"

"We haven't pieced enough together. Before we went to all that work I was going to check with Keel to see if there had been a no trespassing sign or something like that painted on the bridge. We took digital pictures of some of the larger pieces and loaded the images into the computer."

Taylor returned with the laptop. Lopez booted it and turned it toward Sage, who observed, "That Caddy was spray painted and this was done with a brush, but it's the same guy."

"How do you know?"

"Before making a downward stroke, he rises and hooks back. Get the Cocoa Beach PD report. They have photos. He printed 'PERVERT,' the first time, but this doesn't seem to be the same letters."

"We'll piece it together later. I'll get that Cocoa Beach report. Did you see anything that might help identify the guy?"

"Like what?"

"Did you pass any cars in the area....see any tire tracks, lights, hear anything?"

"Not that I can recall right now."

"I'd better see Mr. Keel now. The doctors should be finished with him. Here's my card. Call me if you think of something."

When the deputies left, Sage made another slow trip to the bathroom before taking a nap.

His slumbers were brought to an end by a long face with an asymmetrical grin calling his name.

"Golem. Our savior," said Sage as he moved to shake hands. A big, blue cast canceled that effort, so Sage stuck out his left hand. "Boy, was I glad to see you last night. Without you, we'd probably still be there. How did you manage the helicopter and how did you find us?"

"I was cookin' dinner when your call came in. Of course, you couldn't hear me. I also knew that no ambulance driver could find you, but I was pretty sure I could find the lake from the air. I'd looked it up on a map. I talked air rescue into taking me along. Your 911 call went to Osceola and they didn't know where to go either. What cinched the whole thing was that no one was answering the phone at the Keel ranch. They didn't like it, but they had to take me along as a guide. Of course, they didn't have much of a choice when they learned that a major figure in Florida history was in dire need of medical assistance."

Sage grinned as he dug at the welts on his mosquito ravished face. "If I'd spent any more time out there, I'd have needed a blood transfusion."

Golem laughed. "When I came by earlier, you were asleep, so I went to see Snapper. The detectives were just leaving. He wants to see you. I checked with the head nurse. You can go see him if I push you down in a wheelchair."

"I can walk."

"Probably can, but the doc doesn't want you to, until he's sure all your parts are in the right place and not bruised and swollen. Don't argue." Golem pulled a wheelchair out of the corner and spun it around.

Snapper's room wasn't far away. When Sage pushed the door open, he found a man and a woman seated by the foot of the bed.

"Oh, sorry," said Sage as he motioned with his good arm for Golem to reverse course.

"No, come in," said Snapper. "I want you people to meet. This is my grandson, Clayton, and his wife, Kathy. These are the guys who got me out of that mess. The one with the blue wing is Sage Grayling, my artist. If he hadn't have been with me, I'd still be out there. The one who's 32 hands high is Gordon Lemry....more commonly known as Golem. He's the magician who brought the airborne cavalry. If he hadn't grabbed the reigns, you'd have had the ambulance trailing you into the old ranch house."

Sage could see the family resemblance in build, skin tones, hair and eye color but that was where the similarity ended. Clayton's handshake was firm and brief. On the other hand, Snapper had a firm, but prolonged, friendly handshake as if the contact was important. Clayton stood and even sat straight. He was still wearing a flat top. The old Floridian relaxed and slouched into his surroundings, and he had short hair only after one of his infrequent haircuts.

Kathy was a behavioral duplicate of her husband, except with prominent boobs....*although not in the same league as Tinna.*

"Kathy is trying to talk me into staying at their place until I get back on my feet, but I've decided to stay in Cocoa Beach....close to the doctors and further away from Burke. Golem has said he'd ferry me around."

Kathy made another pitch. "We've doctors up our way too. You could stand some home cooking instead of eating all that restaurant food and trail grub you fix at the ranch."

"Thanks, but I've things to do. Have to replace the Jeep. I'm going back to the one with the rag top. I can slice my way out with my pocket knife. They had to use a can opener to cut me out of that new, fancy thing."

Clay looked at Sage's cast. "If you're right handed, you're not going be doing much painting for a while."

"As soon as the doctors permit, I'll fly back to Albuquerque to take care of some of my own business. When I can handle a brush, I'll return to finish the painting. Snapper said he could put up with my mess until I could swing a brush again."

When the conversation began to drift toward insurance coverage and auto damage, Kathy began to fidget. "Dear, maybe we should let them do their business."

Clay stood. "Perhaps you're right. If you need anything, call us." Clay adjusted his western style hat as if it were a Marine Corps cap.

When the younger Keels were gone, Snapper smiled and shook his head with caution. "Poor Kathy. She's always been afraid of me, but she did her duty and issued the obligatory invitation."

"Your grandson doesn't strike me as the rancher type," said Sage.

"He's not, but he's a first-class officer and he can handle any duty. The ranch is just his current assignment. I own it and when I die, he'll get it. As soon as he gets title, he'll sell the place to round out his retirement."

"That'll be some retirement account," said Golem.

Conversation was cut short with a resounding thump on the door as a very broad, scowling nurse banged her way into the room. "Mr. Keel needs to rest. Out."

There was sufficient intimidation for Golem to grab the handles on the wheelchair and head for the door.

As Sage crawled back into bed he said, "Good. You're going to take care of Snapper."

"He made me an offer I couldn't refuse. He's giving me the keys to the Cadillac to use until he can drive himself. I'll tote him around and pick and fetch."

"If you need it, toss my stuff into a box and the guest room is yours."

"We haven't gotten that far along, but thanks. I'm to drive you to the airport whenever you want to go and pick you up when you return."

Chapter 5

—ᴡᴡ—

Sage was released on the second day. He was able to get a flight out that night. Tinna was to pick him up at the airport. He'd given her only enough information to be assured of some sort of retaliation down the line.

Tinna was never hard to spot. She towered over the normal crowds in her cowboy boots. A quick survey of the crowd would pinpoint her location, even when she was seated. Most everyone reacted to her presence.

Sage had told Tinna he'd gotten beaten up in an auto accident. When she saw the blue cast she seemed uncertain whether she should rant at him or mother him. Temporarily, mothering won out.

For someone 6'4," getting into an MGTD was a little bit of a shoehorn job, but with a heavy arm cast it became more of a chore. Tinna took the opportunity to grouse at him for not telling her about the broken arm. She'd have driven the van instead. Sage ignored her rantings long enough to observe that his cast and Daisy were his junior high school colors. Tinna rolled her eyes up as she slid down behind the wheel. "Okay, Cabron, give. Don't leave out the smallest detail."

Sage gave a broad overview of the events during the ride home, preferring to deal with the details later over a martini. Something was bothering him that needed further consideration.

When they reached the Hacienda, Tinna supervised Sage's ensconcement in his room before tending her kilns.

Half-heartedly Sage sorted through his mail and paid what bills he could on line. He deferred the hand written checks to a later date.

By the time Tinna returned, Sage had the martini makings out and was slowly playing the part of a one-handed bartender.

"Now is the time for you to fill in all the little details you left out," announced Tinna after she had curled up in her overstuffed chair and taken a sip of her martini.

"There are some things that just aren't right about this whole affair. If you don't mind, I'll try talking my way through some of the shady areas."

"Good. Take your time. I've have a pizza to toss in the oven when you're ready."

Sage raised his glass and smiled. "This whole mess started when that graveyard was found on Snapper's land. Almost immediately, Snapper became the prime suspect because of two things....it's his property and he's the only one known to have been around the necessary length of time. At least that is the States Attorneys thinking. As far as I can see, Burke, the SA, has tunnel vision and Snapper is at the end of that tunnel."

"I can see his point, if there is no one else around."

"Just because the graves are on Snapper's property doesn't mean that much."

"Really?"

"Burke has indicated that he suspects Snapper shifted the bodies from the ranch house to the grave site either by horse around the lake or he took the bodies by boat across the lake. I'll bet Burke has never seen that land. It's no easy job getting around the lake. Most of the land on that end of the lake is a bog. And the lake is very shallow. Using a boat, one would have to wade a long ways through the mud to get ashore. Snapper may be tough, but he's not that big."

"Surely, the States Attorney knows that," said Tinna.

"One would think. But I hear he's a city boy. More importantly, it doesn't seem to fit into his agenda."

"You're not a local boy. How is it you know all that stuff?"

"I've seen the topo maps and aerial photos of the ranch. Snapper has them on the walls of the condo. Besides, I've driven through that part of the ranch. It was the bridge over the drainage ditch where the bomb was planted."

"Yes, but who else has access to the ranch and who has been around that long?"

"That's Burke's argument. I doubt if he'll willingly change that point of view, but he may have to try fitting other events into that scenario."

"What are you talking about?" said Tinna as she held her glass up for a refill.

"There have been two attacks on Snapper. The first one was the spray painting of his Caddy. The second was the bridge bomb. Both attacks were the work of the same man."

Tinna cocked her head to the side and raised her eyebrows.

"The guy wrote something on both occasions. He has a quirk of going up before starting a down stroke.

"You know, Cabron, that there is a big difference in painting a car and trying to kill two people."

"He probably wasn't trying to kill me. Usually, Snapper is alone. I was along to help unload a generator."

"That's still a big jump from vandalism to murder."

"Not if you've already murdered twenty times."

"Okay, Pendejo. How did you come to that conclusion?"

"If it had just been a painted car, it could have been an outraged citizen. But I think too much work went into that effort to simply be expressing outrage for an accused action. It took considerable time and energy to find Snapper's habitat and car. That condo is a relatively new acquisition. The Caddy is very new and seldom driven. Also it was not parked in its usual spot. There was a considerable danger of discovery. He had to get in and out of a secured garage area unseen.

"However, that would have been simple compared to finding Snapper's ranch and getting in and out without running a big risk of being trapped in there. Snapper has a very irregular schedule and there aren't many places to hide. Going to all of that trouble brings up other questions."

"Like?"

"Would a morally indignant citizen go to those ends? A relative of one of the murdered men might, but as far as I know none of the identified victims were from around here. And so far, there have not been any bereaved loved ones demanding justice."

"So?"

"So, who would want to see Snapper tried in the press or better yet, die?"

"Hey, Chilito, this is your theory. You tell me."

"If my twenty skeletons had been found but someone else was being targeted as the culprit, I might be inclined to anonymously help the prosecution with its case. I'd be even happier if the prime suspect were to die so the States Attorney could declare the case closed and use his success to win reelection."

"Boy, that sounds as if it's one of your creative projections. Is anyone else on that same brand of gin?"

"It's not so farfetched. I've been around Snapper quite a bit and I haven't come up with even the vaguest feeling of that type of personality quirk. I'm usually pretty sensitive to such inclinations. So, I'm looking at the whole affair from the perspective that Snapper is not involved. If he is out of it, then give me a profile of the killer."

"I don't know anything about the case," protested Tinna.

"You know enough to get started. How old is the killer?"

"How should I know?

"His first victim disappeared in 1948. To have developed a sexual quirk and taken on a World War II vet he'd probably be at least a late teenager. Right?"

"I suppose."

"For the sake of argument, let's use the age of eighteen. So 48 from today's date plus 18 makes our killer in his mid seventies. That's Snapper's age and those are the figures Burke is using to add up to Snapper. But if Snapper didn't do it, then we have a killer out there who also is in his mid-seventies.

"Where do you think he got his victims, if they weren't locals?"

"Why do you say they weren't locals?"

"The sheriff doesn't have any matches for missing persons for those dates. Nor does he have abandoned vehicles with missing drivers for those periods. Where's the easiest place to pick up young males?"

"Hitchhikers?"

"Right, hitchhikers. Guys looking for a car to crawl into. The killer can drive down the road until he finds out if the guy meets his specifications. If he doesn't, then the killer can say that his turn-off is coming up. He dumps the hitchhiker and no one is the wiser. If the guy is nice and juicy......"

"Yuk, Baboso."

"You get the drift. But, in our scenario, he would have to have intimate knowledge of the ranch or at least the burial area. That ridge of dry ground is in dense brush that has been there for decades. He would have had to know the characteristics of the area before wrestling a body all that way into the brush.

"Of course, the killer would need a different approach to the graveyard. He couldn't bring his kill into the ranch house and park there until he buried the body."

Tinna cocked her head to the side before offering, "Maybe he walked his victims in, and then killed them."

"Hadn't thought of that. Could be."

"That would save a lot of hard work."

"Providing he could control the situation," said Sage. "He'd have a hard time trying to get me to walk to my grave. Besides, I think the killer probably had his fun and games elsewhere and the victim would not be any condition for a hike. Then there is the situation that each body was wrapped in a blanket. The chances are the body was quite bloody. The blanket probably covered up the bloody mess."

"Yuk."

Sage continued his line of thought. "Our killer has been around for decades, although not in the immediate vicinity of the ranch. Snapper should know him and probably will eventually make the connection."

Tinna held up the olive on the toothpick like a diminutive baton. "You're missing some considerations."

"Yes?"

"Maybe Snapper knows the guy, but doesn't have reason to make such a connection. On the other hand, your killer may have gained knowledge of the ranch at one time, but lives somewhere else and only comes back to dispose of his lovers. However, my favorite scenario is that this is a cult burial ground for their ceremonial victims." Tinna smiled sweetly as she held up her glass for a refill.

"You really know how to screw up a guy's carefully crafted theories." As payback Sage made a real production of maneuvering his bruised and broken body out of the overstuffed chair to fulfill her request.

It was Sage's turn to smile. "Well, I have to admit those are scenarios that I hadn't considered. If this case is still open when I get back to Cocoa Beach, I'll steal them to muddy Burke's case."

After Sage's exaggerated broken-wing display, Tinna lapsed back into her mothering mode that included dinner and tucking him into bed at an early hour. Apparently, Tinna didn't want to risk being beaten to death with his blue cast, so she headed for her own apartment.

Day-by-day, the soreness became history. The itch was still there. The local doctors said the arm was coming along well. As Sage felt better, his frustration grew. He'd always been an active, physical creature and any infirmities were intolerable. There was a long list of projects to be done around the Hacienda, but most of them required two hands or at least a right hand. To keep from completely losing it, he hired Manuel, a young Chicano metal worker who had a long work history on the Hacienda reconstruction. Because of his Mexican heritage, Manuel figured that the Hacienda was actually his and Sage was only a temporary tenant.

With only one wing, Sage could still supervise and Manuel could do most anything that Sage could dream up. If Manuel needed any additional muscle, he had a raft of cousins to lend a hand.

In addition to the daytime diversion, Tinna took it upon herself to aid the night rehabilitating of Sage's stamina. Despite all the efforts of his friends, Sage kept fretting about his unfinished painting and Snapper's predicament. He spent considerable time on the phone with Snapper and Golem.

Snapper was making a good recovery. Due to his age, he lost the pain and stiffness much slower than Sage. When Sage talked with him, the rancher was invariably positive about his own condition and also unconcerned about Burke's investigation.

However, the picture changed somewhat when Sage was able to talk with Golem on his home phone. Sage sensed that Golem's answers were not completely forthcoming when Snapper was around. Sage called Golem at home and left a message on the answering machine.

When Golem called back, the two engaged in some introductory small talk before Sage said, "I get the feeling your comments are somewhat censored when Snapper is around."

Golem laughed. "Was I that obvious?"

It was Sage's turn to laugh. "You were only obvious enough to raise my antennae to get me to call. What's up? Isn't Snapper recovering properly?"

"Oh, he's recovering, but not as quickly as he thinks he should. Of course, his time schedule is based on his recuperative powers forty years ago. He wants to push it too fast.

"However, the main problem is why he's pushing his rehab. He's developed a real vendetta against whoever planted that bomb. Snapper wants to be ready to confront him, mano-a-mano, as soon as he can figure out who did it."

"Does he have any idea who planted the bomb?"

"Not yet, but he's beginning to turn over all the rocks in central Florida and poke a stick into every bush. He's got all the private detectives in the area on his payroll.

"Then the other day," continued Golem, "Jake called to invite Snapper over for a steak. When I showed up with Snapper, Jake wondered where you were."

"Did Jake have anything on his mind?"

"Yep. Jake had been getting reports that a big time real estate developer had shown a lot of interest in Snapper's ranch. He'd been driving around the area, flying over it and getting county maps. None of this particularly surprised Jake because developers have always been eying that general area for years. The territory closer to Kissimmee is much lower and swampier. What caused Jake to call Snapper was that there seems to be a relationship between the developer and David Burke.

"Oh, boy. How did Snapper take that news?"

"Not well. Snapper's imagination is running wild. He's building all sorts of mountains. Now he thinks there may be a conspiracy to get his ranch. He's installed a rifle rack in his new Jeep. And he's saddle soaped his old buscadero belt and oiled his ancient brace of Peacemaker .45 Colts.

That brought a chuckle from Sage. Being a visually oriented type, he immediately built a marvelous image.

"You laugh," accused Golem. "This is no laughing matter."

"Oh, I know it isn't, but what a marvelous opportunity Fredrick Remington missed."

Even Golem had to acknowledge that marvelous image, but he quickly returned to the serious considerations at hand. "When are you coming back? I could use some help."

"What help could I be with a broken wing? The cast doesn't come off for a week."

"I don't mean physical help. It's your moral authority that is needed."

"Moral authority?"

"You know what I mean. I've always been known as the town clown. No one takes what I say seriously. You're known as a deep, serious thinker. You and Snapper have already gotten hurt, but with the massing of firepower, it looks as if there might be some fatalities. Snapper has a very serious reputation behind him."

Sage paused for a moment. "I hadn't planned on coming back until I could swing a brush, which I hear will be a while after the cast comes off. I'm not much good around here. Maybe I'll return and have the cast removed there. Besides I have some new thoughts about the killer."

"Please give it some serious consideration. Much of the future is in question right now."

"What would Snapper think if I came back early?"

"He doesn't know when 'early' would be. He keeps talking about your return. I'll meet you at the airport whenever you say."

Chapter 6

—m—

Tinna gave him a begrudging early sendoff. Golem offered up an over-exuberant welcome and Snapper seemed to pick up in mid-sentence as if there had been no absence. Sage's painting material hadn't even picked up any dust, due to the filtered A/C system.

Sage had to juggle his property around in the guest room. Golem had returned home since Snapper needed only occasional services. A new, older style Jeep with a cloth top sat next to Dreadnought. Sage noted the locked gun rack behind the seat.

At Sage's request, Golem had made an appointment for the cast to be removed. The reminder card was on the bed. The removal was a long awaited event. The cast was hot, itchy and stinky.

After Sage refeathered his nest, he found Golem perched on his viewing stool in the dining room. "I'm ready for you to add a few strokes. I've memorized these."

Sage laughed, "I'll bet you have. After the cast comes off tomorrow I'll be able to see how stiff I am and what kind of shakes I have. I may have to go to a stronger mall stick."

The phone rang. Snapper was sitting at the card table in the library area at the end of the living room next to the master bedroom.

The conversation was virtually monosyllabic, "Yeah, okay, okay, no, yeah, continue."

Snapper made notations on the top sheet of what looked like a ream of paper. When he finished, he dropped the sheet into a hanging folder in a crate-file box beside the table.

As Sage was scowling at the dried oils on his palette, Snapper announced, "I'm buying dinner at Jake's tonight. I'm going to take a nap before bourbon-time."

Snapper turned off the phone ringer and shut himself in the master bedroom.

As Sage dug out his single-edged razor blade holder to scrape his glass palette, he said, "I haven't done a lick of work since the accident and I suspect you haven't had time to do much carving either."

"I haven't done much carving, but business has been great."

"Really?"

"There's a world of busy-bodies out there. I'm now associated with a famous or infamous character and the best way to get into a conversation with me is to want to buy one of my pieces. I had a fair inventory, but now I'm just taking names and substantial deposits."

"I hope your prices have gone up. You were practically giving those pieces away."

All Sage got was a crooked smile that wasn't as striking as when Golem had his eye shadow on. After a pause, Golem continued, "There's been another business change. Snapper has given me space in the stables to do my work. There's an enclosed feed room where I can put a bunk if I want to stay over. Also I can have all the palms I need. There are hundreds of dead palms scattered around the ranch. I can use an old Ford Ferguson tractor and trailer to get the logs."

"Great," said Sage with feeling. "You've been in need of space. Can you get by without electricity?"

"The only power tool I use now is the drill to make the hole for the pipe. I can do that at the apartment as I do now or I can use a brace and bit and do it by hand. That's no problem."

"It sounds like a good deal. Snapper will benefit too by having someone else around to help fight off the Indian attacks."

"Yeah, I figure it wouldn't be a bad idea to have someone else coming and going around the property. Ya can't plant another bomb and be assured the right guy will drive over it."

"Are you assuming the bomber really cares?"

"Oh, oh." said Golem.

The pair chatted until the sun dropped far enough to flood the dining room with hot light. That roused Snapper, who appeared, yelling "cocktail time." That started a general exodus to the kitchen. As Sage and Snapper were building their respective drinks, Golem pulled a Coors longneck out of the refrigerator.

Snapper plunked down in one of the easy chairs in the living room instead of heading for the patio. He shook his head before saying, "All these new conveniences are making a wimp out of me. Before I moved in here, I never even thought about the humidity. Now look at me."

"No sense in banging yourself on the head with a bung starter when you don't have to," said Golem.

Sage wasn't displeased that he could avoid the humidity. The high heat of Albuquerque was much more tolerable. As the trio settled in for the evening happy hour, Sage debated about tossing out his recent thoughts concerning the killer. However, those considerations were put aside by Snapper, who took it upon himself to bring Sage up-to-date on the roadside bomb investigation. "That Deputy Lopez, who talked to you before you left, said your idea about both the bomb and the spray paint job being done by the same character was right on. When they pieced the bridge together it became evident that even though the bastard tried to make it look as if it was a different person doing the lettering, it was the same guy."

"That would indicate the guy wants everyone to think there is more than one person after you," said Sage. "What else did they find out?"

"Very little for sure. They found a tire mark, but it's a standard Goodyear tire used on lots of new cars and sold everywhere. It was a very new tire without any distinguishing marks. It was a poor print. Anything that was left at the bridge, blew up."

"How about the explosives?"

"Ammonium nitrate fertilizer with diesel oil in a plastic sack. They only found bits and pieces of the detonator, but not enough to tell too much about it other than it was a crude device."

"Can you get into the farmhouse without a long walk?"

"Oh, yes, there are several approaches to the house if you know your way around. Clay sent a ranch crew out the next day. They dragged in another log and put on a new deck. I'm back in business."

"When do they think the bomb was planted?"

Snapper shook his head. "They don't know."

"I'd guess it was between 7:30 and 9:00 that morning."

Both Snapper and Golem gave Sage a skeptical look. In defense of his position, Sage offered up his thinking. "He had to check if you'd stayed the night in town or on the ranch. If you were on the ranch he couldn't do it without running the risk of being seen. If you stayed here, then if you maintained your normal schedule, you wouldn't be out there until around 10:00 am. That's predicated on your getting up at your usual time, having coffee, reading the newspaper, going out to eat and then traveling your normal route.

"He could check if your Jeep was at the condo around dawn. Unless he was intimately familiar with the ranch road, he'd wait until daylight. It shouldn't take him too long to plant the bomb and set the trip, if everything was prepared ahead. If he could get out by 9:00 he'd be out to the main road before you'd arrive, even if you were running early."

Golem shrugged and said to Snapper, "You know what's so sad? He's probably right."

"Yeah, it's that fussy painter mind. He has too long to think. Come on, let's go eat."

With two sets of very long legs, the trio chose a table over a booth.

When Jake arrived, they got the double finger pointing, which added a fourth.

After all the initial small talk was completed and the dinner orders placed, Jake tossed out an interesting question, "Say, Snapper, how many acres have you got in that ranch of yours?

After a moment, that Sage couldn't accredit to uncertainty or hesitancy in divulging the information, Snapper said, "Oh, 150,000 plus or minus."

"I hear it's quite a bit plus."

"Where'd you hear that?"

"A couple of guys from the Osceola County Clerk's office were having dinner last night. I just happened to be sitting at the next booth and when I heard your name, I bent a little ear in their direction. It seems that someone is making inquires about your holdings. Those guys were bitterly complaining about trying to figure out what you own and how you got it."

Snapper laughed. "I can see where that could be a problem."

"How so?" asked Sage.

"Back in the old days property lines were between one tree and another or the corner of a lake. Later on they started rudimentary surveys, which really didn't match up. Originally, my granddad claimed a tract of land. Later, when dad started buying more land, he also claimed any chinks in between. I continued acquiring land and I did the same thing. And the tax collector was more than happy to charge me taxes for every acre."

"Apparently," said Jake, "they are concerned about how all those bits and pieces can be conveyed without any kickbacks when it's subdivided."

Jake paused. He looked at Snapper expectantly as if he was seeking an answer to a question he didn't want to ask.

"It wasn't me. I have no plans to split up the ranch. It's no secret my grandson, Clay, will get the ranch. There must be another game in town to which I haven't been invited."

Golem squirmed in his chair trying to get the kinks out of his legs. Both Sage and Snapper waited for him to settle down. They recognized the signs. Golem didn't often offer gratuitous gossip without some fidgeting first. "I've heard rumors that our friend, David Burke, has been getting a lot of attention from Arnold Hampton, a big-time developer in the attractions area. Hampton arranged for Burke's membership in Arendale Country Club. That's a pretty upscale place for a states attorney. They don't make all that much money."

"Every time I turn around I keep running into that Burke. Yesterday I was talking with Hack, who says Burke doesn't want to sign a complaint against me because if anything goes wrong, the Appaloosa Apple could land in his lap. Hack seems to think he'll take the case to the grand jury. Now, why would a developer be cozying up to Burke?"

"An ornery old critter like you," said Jake "could hang around until you're a hundred and twenty. Maybe Burke could hasten the execution of your will."

Snapper slowly rotated his long neck bottle in its sweat-ring. "Then Hampton would have to deal with Clay. Yep, there's another game in town."

Chapter 7

—m—

It was a distinct relief to get the cast removed. However, Sage found that he was very protective of his mended wing. The first exercise, when he got back to the condo, was to see how he could handle a brush. He was rather disgruntled over how shaky he was. It would be a while before he was back to the minute detail work with a three-hair bush.

Snapper didn't seem to be concerned that there would be further delays before Sage was capable of full capacity work.

Snapper was pretty much back to his old self. He wasn't depending on Golem, except on infrequent occasions. The repainted Caddy had gone back into its parking space after Golem brought Sage back from the doctor's office. Since Golem was in his working eye paint, Sage figured he was prospecting again.

The next morning, Snapper didn't go out for breakfast. He wanted to be on the road early. Before leaving, he said he'd be back for cocktails.

Sage spent the day giving his work area a thorough cleaning. He laid out a fresh palette and did some background fill-in. It was not a satisfying effort. Golem never showed up to liven the pathetic day.

When Snapper returned in the late afternoon, he was in a subdued mood, which matched Sage's.

"I might hazard a guess that your day wasn't much better than mine," said Sage.

"Oh, you'd think by this time I'd realize other people don't view the world through my eyes. I went out to see my grandson. When I got there Kathy wasn't home. I asked after her. Clay said she was at the country club. I said that I didn't know that they belonged to a country club. It wasn't a secret....just a recent development. He went on to explain that a friend, Arnold Hampton, had helped them get a membership.

"Arnold Hampton, the developer?"

"I asked the same question. It was. This set up the best man-to-man talk I've ever had with Clay. It was good, but hard....really hard, when reality set in.

"Everyone knows Clay is in line to inherit the Circle K. It is also apparent to anyone who knows ranching, that Clay is no rancher. He can do a respectable job on any assigned duty. This ranch is an assignment. The duration of that duty is until I die.

"Eventually, that land will come on the market. Hampton is one of the shrewdest developers around. He thinks a long way ahead. He came to Clay and Kathy and made them a business offer. He wants the right of first refusal when the ranch comes up for sale. For that right there was a cash amount, but the real clincher was a membership in the Arendale Country Club.

"Clay explained something to me that had never crossed my mind. He said all their married life Clay and Kathy knew that they would eventually be millionaires. The only question was when. Being a military wife is no posy-patch. Besides the built-in hazards of death and maiming associated with the service, there is a lot of moving around. Even though the government picks up a lot of the freight, it still costs the families a bundle. An officer's wife has a bunch of duties beyond her immediate family. There are volunteer duties and social obligations, which require money. She was always trying to get her dollars to stretch far enough to cover everything. For thirty years money was tight.

"With Clay's retirement and the income from the ranch, there's a lot more money, but Kathy is still stuck out in the sticks outside a small town. Kathy wants to enjoy life in a way only money will make possible. Clay is afraid Kathy will be too old to enjoy the millions once they get here.

"I have more money than I'll ever need. Clay's mother is fixed in the lifestyle she has chosen. So I've asked Hack to find the least tax painless way to transfer the ranch to Clay. He can do as he sees fit."

Sage sat in silence for a bit before saying, "It's going to be tough seeing your granddad's, dad's and your whole life's work become rows of ticky-tacky."

"I'm going to do some subdividing of my own. I'm going to section off about a hundred and twenty acres around the old ranch house plus access from the county road. I'll also divide off my daughter-in-law's house and put it in her name. I'm also going to bring electricity to the old house."

"Snapper, you're getting soft."

A big grin spread across the old rancher's weathered face. "Ain't it grand? Let's see if happy hour can cheer us up."

After the pair returned to the living room with their drinks, Sage inquired, "Have you figured out why your developer has been also wining and dining Burke?"

"No, but when I no longer have the ranch, Burke's services might no longer be needed. That might piss Burke off," said Snapper with a leer.

"Piss him off too much and he might engage in precipitous action he might normally avoid."

"Good. That's when I've found people get careless."

"You know," said Sage, "that the guy that booby-trapped the bridge may not be finished yet."

"You're probably right. I've spent a bundle of money hiring people to track the bastard down and I have absolutely nothing to show for it. All I can do now is to be vigilant and try to be prepared."

"One other thing." Sage proceeded to tell Snapper of his thoughts concerning the identity of the assailant....that he is also the killer. "And I'll bet you there is some connection between the two of you, which would make it possible for you to identify him if you could only remember it."

"So you think my dementia is getting in the way. You know, you're not helping me sleep at night."

****

Day-by-day Sage regained his painting control. Golem had moved his carving operation to the ranch, so he was out of Cocoa Beach a lot. He would, as time allowed, drop in to check the progress of the painting. And occasionally they'd meet at the Beach Shanty for beers.

One evening, Sage found a bathing suit-clad Arty Misconi drinking beer with Golem. "Hey, Arty. Aren't you out of uniform?"

"No, I don't normally work weekends."

"Oh, what day is this?"

"Sunday."

"Really, I missed the NASCAR races again."

"Yeah, it was up at Daytona this weekend. My boss will be there posing as a he-man."

"Really, how does that little whiff do that?"

"Oh, he finds ways. Burke has a clear plastic cube on his desk that holds five pictures. Each Monday morning, the first item of business is to change the pictures. He has two drawers of his desk completely full of photographs."

"Pictures of what?" said Sage.

"Oh, it depends on the season. If it's duck hunting season he'll have five poses of him sticking a fancy 12 gauge shotgun out of a blind, taking a duck from the mouth of a Golden Retriever, standing with a gun slung across his shoulder or holding up a string of ducks.

"He's got tons of fishing pictures fighting marlin, catching tarpon, holding up oversized reds....whatever is available. He owns a fancy horse so there are a lot of him and horsey pictures. This weekend it will be muscle cars and famous drivers."

"How does he come up with all those photos?" said Sage.

"His mother and younger brother are his official photographers. I don't pay much attention to that."

"What does he do with all those pictures?" said Sage.

"The cube is on the front of his desk. He always has some sort of entrée to be able to draw the photos to the attention of whoever ventures into his office. He has to prove to himself and everyone else that even though he's a little shit, he's still a real man."

It was abundantly apparent to Sage that Arty had not been converted by all the propaganda. "How does Burke respond to challenges?"

"Ha! He takes on all comers if the challenge involves skills or endurance. He's not about to arm wrestle with you or take you on shooting hoops. Then he shamelessly plays the size card. Boy, am I glad I don't have to fight those battles."

A tiny idea was beginning to take root and Sage wanted to nurture it without further material distractions, so he changed the subject. "So you're a surfer. Not much opportunity for that where I come from."

"Where's that?" asked Arty.

"Albuquerque."

"That I can believe."

The next day Snapper left for the ranch. Golem was there too. Sage went through the phone numbers Snapper had jotted down in the margins of the phone book cover. He found Hack's office number, but if what Snapper had said was true, he wouldn't be there. There was also a cell phone number. Sage dialed it.

"Lo? What do you want, Snapper?"

"Hack, this is Sage Grayling, Snapper's painter. I've got an idea I'd like to run by you."

"When?'

"Anytime. Snapper's at the ranch, so today would be a good time."

"Oh, that kind of idea, huh? In an hour I'll be sitting in the boot black stand in the Cowhunter Saloon on Hwy 17. Can't miss it. They lost their liquor license so it's now one of those froufrou coffee houses, but they never redecorated."

"I'm tall and I'll be wearing cowboy boots."

"Don't use 'boy' around here. You might insult someone bigger than you."

Sage laughed. "I'll remember that."

Five minutes later Dreadnought emerged from the garage into the glaring Florida sun. Hack had been right. He couldn't have missed the Cowhunter Saloon if he had tried. It was as unique as Snapper's ranch and about the same vintage. An unpaved parking lot was covered with what Sage had been told was Marl when he had first seen the white surface material. It was a local, natural product that when compacted was a hard as concrete. Sage suspected that the hitching rail under the old, faded sign was for show. But, then, it might just have been a newer replacement of original equipment, because it fit right into the scene.

It took a moment for his eyes to adjust to the dim interior light. There was an old brass railed bar looping from the left and disappearing into the gloom to the rear. The rest of the room beyond the bar was filled with round poker tables and wooden chairs. The chrome espresso machine and a phalanx of bottles were completely incongruous, as were the two cute little blondes behind the bar. Across the room from the bar was a six-place, elevated bootblack stand. The seat closest to the front door was occupied by a duplicate of Snapper. They didn't look the same in the face, but dress, posture and actions were out of the same crucible.

Hack patted the seat to his right. "You got younger eyes than me. You can look into the light."

As the two shook hands, Hack said, "I think I'm going to like you. At least I like your horse." He jerked his head toward Dreadnought.

Sage surveyed the saloon interior from his high perch. "What a fabulous painting this would make."

"I'm glad they didn't tear the building down. I have a lot of memories associated with this old place. Hack slapped the arm of his seat. "This has been my primary office for thirty years. I've settled more cases here than I ever did in any courtroom."

Hack signaled one of the girls. "Do you drink coffee or do you want one of those frothy things?"

"Black coffee."

"Two mugs of dark, honey."

When the coffee was served, Hack settled back in his seat, balanced his mug on the arm and carefully placed his boots on the metal stands. "I presume you want to talk about Snapper," said the attorney before he took a tentative sip to test the temperature of the coffee.

"Yeah, I believe that Snapper has nothing to do with those bodies and that the murderer is still out there. I think both attacks, the car paint job and the bomb, were the work of the real murderer and that Snapper is in jeopardy because the guy will try again."

"So far we're thinking alike."

"As I see it, right now our big problem is the States Attorney. He thinks he's got his killer and therefore no one is looking elsewhere."

"We're still on the same page. Outside of delivering the murderer to Burke, what would you suggest we do?"

"I've always had reservations concerning diminutive males. They keep having to prove themselves and ultimately they have a desperate need to win. From what I hear Burke leads that category of males. I was thinking we might use that proclivity to shoot some holes in his theory."

"Continue."

"I hear he is claiming that it would be a simple thing for Snapper to bring those boys to the ranch, have his fun and then kill them. All Snapper would have to do is throw the bodies over a pack horse and trot over to the graveyard or toss the bodies in a boat and row across the lake to the burial site.

"I've been to the ranch and I've seen maps and photos of the area. That's no simple trip."

"Yes, I know. That will be part of the defense if it comes to trial."

"I understand Burke is a city boy, but he features himself a horseman. Why not use that part of your defense to blow holes in his theory before it goes to court? Maybe we can get him off his pet theory so he'll look elsewhere. I was thinking of challenging Burke to accompany me, if he's man enough, to ride to the graveyard. I should be able to get a mount and pack horse from Snapper. I'll even let Burke ride his own horse instead of having to deal with a breachy little Florida mustang."

Hack thought for a bit. Finally, he shook his head. "Burke wouldn't go for it for two reasons. You're too big and an out-of-towner. You embody too many unknowns. But on the other hand he couldn't very well pass up a challenge from an old, local attorney." Hacker smiled wickedly.

"This may solve another problem," continued Hack. "I'm having a hard time keeping our friend from sticking a Colt .45 up Burke's left nostril or any other available orifice and challenging him to a direct confrontation. I keep telling him that a .45 is too big. It wouldn't fit. Besides, that's not how things get done these days. On any one-on-one meeting, Snapper would win initially, but he'd lose in the end when the law would send an army after him. That army would not make any value judgment, but only do their assigned duty."

"I know what you mean," said Sage. "That attitude is winning out in my area too. Anyone with a highly developed sense of right and wrong and a personal sense of duty is considered to be a dangerous person who must be watched."

"How come as young a feller as you knows that?"

"I've never painted an electric guitar, an iPod, a stun gun, stiletto heels....any of those things. But I've painted a lot of wooden guitars, violins, antique Colts and Remingtons and battered cow 'hunter' boots. And as slowly as I paint, I have a lot of time to consider my subjects."

Hack finished his coffee. "Let me think on this a while. In ten minutes I'll be sitting in your seat with a guy on both sides of me. I'll be settling a riparian rights question. So scat."

Chapter   8

Sage forgot about his arm. He could lose himself in his painting. Golem dropped in occasionally to check on the progress. One morning, he let himself in considerably earlier than normal. Sage was still in the breakfast room dawdling over his coffee and the newspaper. Snapper had spent the night at the ranch.

Golem came in with an oversized crooked smile that threatened to break out in full bloom laughter. "I just got a call from Arty. Have you heard what happened last night at the Grand Cypress, the big resort hotel?"

"No."

"Last night there was a big Democratic fund raiser. All sort of bigwigs assembled to tell the moneyed people how good their candidates are. The local candidates were present, trying to get their feet in the trough.

"During the post-dinner meet-and-greet sessions someone asked Hack, who was one of the money-men in attendance, about representing Snapper Keel in that mass murder case. Of course, that was after the dinner wine and the complimentary drinks had been going on for some time. Old Hack is getting a little hard of hearing, so the guy had to repeat the question in a louder voice.

"Hack came back with a dismissive answer to the effect that the states attorney was just making election year political hay. He continued by saying that Burke didn't have a case because he didn't know what he was talking about. Then Hack said, "Ya can't expect a tiny feller like that to be able to see the fallacies in his fantasy.

"The guy asked what he was talking about. Hack went on to ridicule Burke's theory on how the killer would be able to sling his victim on a pack horse and take it around the lake to the burial ground or toss it in a boat to row it across for disposal. He said, 'I'd love to see him demonstrate that theory but, of course, when one has to deal with under-sized males, things get difficult.'

"At that moment Burke stepped around a big potted plant. He was livid and shouted, 'If you want to talk about me, do it to my face. I can do anything you can do.'

"It couldn't have been better if it had been staged," said Golem.

Sage smiled.

"Anyway, Hack looked Burke over from head to toe and just smiled, which made Burke madder. Burke shouted again, "I can do anything you can do."

Hack said in a rather dismissive way that if Burke knew how to ride, he'd have Burke demonstrate the body disposal techniques he's been advancing over TV. Burke stuck out his Bantam chest and he stated he could ride just as good as Hack and he'd prove his theory if Hack wasn't too old to make such a ride.

"Hack asked if Burke had his own horse or should Hack provide one. The SA replied that he had a very good horse, not like those old broom-tails they ride in Florida.

"So Hack said, 'I'll meet you at 7:00 am on Sunday at Snapper's ranch. You know where it is. You spent enough time pawing through his things. I'll provide the pack horse and body."

An enormous crowd had gathered and as Hack started to push his way through, Burke yelled, "I'll be there old man." Burke had to jump to see over the crowd to make his parting shot at Hack. How delicious it must have been."

Sage decided not to alter a perfect story. Also he didn't want even the hint of a setup to get back to Burke, so he said, "Does Snapper know of this?"

"Not from me," said Golem, "but I bet it won't be long before the big challenge hits the morning news on both radio and television. When he leaves the ranch, he'll catch it on the car radio."

Sage had a new language on his Walkman....Icelandic. When Tinna got mad she lapsed into talking to herself into her native language. Sage had thought it would be fun to understand what she was saying although he would emphatically deny he knew a single word in the language. Icelandic was no cream puff and he was getting frustrated. After Golem's visit he had reason to suspend the language lessons while he mentally investigated the various scenarios that the Hack challenge had opened.

In mid-afternoon, Snapper came stomping in. He'd heard the report of the challenge and of course went hunting for Hack, whom he finally found at his grandson's place, arranging for horses to be delivered to the old ranch house. He'd gotten Kathy to sew a piece of canvas saddlebags so it would carry a couple of 80 pound sacks of cement. It was to be thrown over a pack horse to simulate a body.

Snapper was not a happy camper. He didn't like for others to carry his water and to top it off, Hack had ordered him to stay away from the ranch. The order included Sage. Hack wanted to be the sole source of information.

All Saturday, the challenge was hyped by the local media. It even made the cable news channels that had picked up the story when the graves were discovered.

Sunday morning arrived clear and bright. Sage rolled out of bed to catch the early morning news. Snapper already had the coffee made. He was still grumbling about Hack making the challenge. "He's an old man. He shouldn't be horning in on my responsibilities."

"What are you talking about? Hack's your attorney. You pay him to act in your behalf. And another thing, you're older than he is."

Snapper quibbled, "Only by four months."

There was a TV truck at the ranch house. When the coverage began, Hack was dressed in old work clothes with battered boots and a misshapen straw hat. He was sitting on the top rail of a corral fence. Two small Florida horses were tied to the fence. One had a well-worn western saddle and the other had the canvas bag with the cement sacks slung across its back.

Hack was watching the Burke entourage unload a handsome black horse from a fancy trailer. Two photographers were busy getting cube pictures. Burke had two horse handlers dealing with the black. There were also two deputy states attorneys watching their boss prepare.

Hack waved off an ever increasing gaggle of reporters. Burke was occupied supervising his horse handlers on saddling the black. Finally, in his fashionable riding habit and highly polished boots, he got a leg up to mount.

Hack stepped off the fence into the saddle, unfastened the lead rope and joined the States Attorney. Hack pointed toward the gravesite across the lake and then gestured to the adjacent shore line, indicating that Burke should lead the way. Hack handed Burke the pack horse lead.

On TV, it didn't look all that far across the lake, and the end of the lake was clearly visible.

The black, an American Saddle-bred, high stepper, pranced off at a brisk pace. Hack tagged along behind. Media cars followed at a distance.

"Ha!" snorted Snapper. "Those guys haven't the foggiest idea of where they're going. If they drive, they need 4-wheelers or, better yet, a mud buggy."

The high boom on the TV truck was able to follow their progress. The expeditionary force hadn't gone two hundred yards before the horses started throwing water about. Burke had to veer to the right to get out of the muck.

"In a little bit, Burke will hit dry ground. He'll follow it out to the end of a peninsula and then have to backtrack further to the right than he is now. It won't be long until those sedans will be bogged down."

"How much of that soft ground is there?" asked Sage.

"This is the beginning of our rainy season. It would take them less time to ride to the cemetery if they'd stuck to the road and ridden around to the road that goes in to the cattle pens, which are on the other side of the lake. It's a long way around but quicker."

As the horses moved out of range of the TV truck, there wasn't anything to show. The commentator didn't have anyone to interview other than Burke's mother and brother and the two horse handlers. The TV truck changed locations giving them a distant view of the horsemen. The cars were already stuck and their occupants were slogging back to high ground. A call had gone out for ATVs, but they didn't arrive until three hours into the trip. The horsemen still hadn't rounded the end of the lake.

Snapper was enjoying himself. He had his feet propped up while he sipped coffee. Even at the great distance from the TV camera, he could see Burke was in trouble. "That black is floundering. He won't last much longer. He's used up all his vinegar."

Sure enough, twenty minutes later Burke headed toward the road.

"He should have given up two hours ago," declared Snapper. "His horse has just gone lame."

Sage shifted his attention to the black. It took him a while to spot the limp on the right front.

"At least that stupid bastard is showing some consideration for his horse." Burke had slipped off the black and was leading him out. One of the ATVs arrived with a horse handler. Burke turned his horse over to the handler and climbed onto the back of the ATV.

"I wonder if this little episode will change Burke's mind about how easy it would be to get to the burial ground from your ranch." said Sage.

"Oh, he'll probably just figure I didn't use that route. He'll just start looking for the real route."

The pair watched the TV news coverage of the challenge. Burke wasn't admitting defeat because there were intervening factors. He said he'd called it off because his horse had strained a leg and he also complained that it would have been different if he had known the lay of the land.

After the news Sage said, "That little episode didn't change his mind. Maybe it will slow him down a bit while he dreams up another way to get the bodies to the burial ground. The TV coverage made him look foolish."

"Yeah," said Snapper with an evil grin. "And the media backs him. Think of what they'd have said if they were on the other side of the political fence."

Chapter 9

—ɯ—

The phone woke Sage before his alarm clock. Snapper had taken the call, but he was bellowing for Sage to pick up.

It was Hack. He started giving Sage instructions after he told Snapper to hang up. "You be at the Cowhunter Saloon at 9:40 at the latest. Take the second seat on the boot-black stand. The management will put reserved signs up. I'll be there at 10:00 and sit on the end. The media will be there to grill me on the ride. I want you to shield me from the right and maybe to give me a hand up onto the stand. I'm so stiff and sore it hurts to open my eyes. It was your idea that put me in this condition, so you can ride shotgun. I don't want to see Snapper there and you don't need to tell him how stove up I am."

Sage could hear Snapper loading the coffee pot, so Sage gave up on trying to get a few more winks.

"What's that old coot want?" was Sage's greeting in the kitchen.

"He's setting the stage for the media at the Cowhunter Saloon. I'm running shotgun so he can control the situation and not get caught up in it."

"And he doesn't want me there."

Sage smiled. "How'd you guess?"

Since he'd rather be early than late, Sage arrived at the saloon.... come coffee house, thirty-five minutes early. There was a strip of cash register tape across the seats of the boot black stand with a reserved sign taped to the first seat.

The girl at the espresso machine recognized Sage and waved him to the stand. She asked what he wanted.

"Dark, in a mug."

When the coffee came, Sage started to reach for money, but the girl waived him off. "Hack has a tab."

Sage was none too early. The first of the media people arrived along with his mug of coffee. Since no one recognized him, Sage was able to eavesdrop on some of the developing conversations. The general attitude that was being exhibited was that Burke had made a fool of himself by accepting such a challenge in the first place and then in the second place being unable to physically demonstrate the feasibility of one of his primary theories. Although this opinion held consensus, there were indications that the editorial policies of the various media outlets would not tolerate too harsh a criticism. As the time approached for Hack's appearance, there was a flurry of activity by the camera crews setting up out front for first glimpses.

When Hack arrived, he came in the back door while the news people were gathered about the front entry wanting to get in the first question.

Hack made his way along the bar and across to the boot-black stand before anyone spotted him. He swung the steel boot stand aside and extended his left hand to Sage. With a tug from Sage, Hack swung into the seat before the throng arrived.

"Thanks," said Hack, "I needed that."

As the clamor started, Hack raised his hand. "Let that pretty girl with my coffee get through. You don't want to talk to me until I've had my coffee."

A pretty young woman tore that paper tape away from the seat next to Sage while trying to lean across Sage to get her recorder into Hack's face. Since Hack had asked him to ride shotgun, the painter figured it was to protect him from assault such as this. So, Sage waited until the next jostle came along. He sloshed his hot dark roast coffee all down the front of the woman's cream colored suit. As the female reporter squealed, Sage howled "My coffee" and glowered as the dark stain expanded from the chest into her lap. The damaged reporter jumped off the stand to get out of view of the running cameras.

Sage held his mug up indicating he wanted a refill before turning his attention back to Hack's interview. The timber of the questions seemed to have a political undertone that Hack had been trying to embarrass the states attorney to damage his political career.

Hack argued that the event was to demonstrate the complete and utter fallacy of Burke's murder scenario. He strongly contended that the exercise demonstrated the states attorney's position was completely untenable.

Since the media wasn't getting fodder for its desired agenda, there was a gradual withdrawal.

When the throng dwindled to three persistent print reporters, Hack said, "Okay, guys. I have some lawyering to do now. You'll have to fake the rest."

After the final departure, Hack said, "Thanks for the hand-up. I'm so stove-up I'd have had to crawl up. I haven't spent that much time in the saddle in years, but don't tell Snapper." Then Hack chuckled. "At least I don't have a handful of blisters, a lame horse and ruined pair of expensive riding boots."

"How's that?"

"Burke was riding an English saddle with no horn. He had to drag the balky pack horse all the way. I just made a loop and tossed the rope over the horn."

"I saw his horse go lame over the TV."

"They showed that on TV?"

"It was a long shot but if you know anything about horses you could tell what was happening. Snapper spotted it first."

Hack grinned. "Burke pulled a sole off one of those fancy, shiny boots. They're not made for slogging through muck. Hope his horse wasn't seriously injured."

Sage shrugged. "I hope it was his ego that was injured. But, I hope it was not serious enough to blind him to the reality that his theory is full of holes."

"Burke is a smart little coyote. He probably knows the flaws in his disposal theory. Our problem is that we're running the risk of rage blinding him to those shortcomings. I received word that he ranted and raved all the way home. There are other ramifications to his humiliation. His political career could be in jeopardy. He needs a conviction."

"Maybe he'll look elsewhere for a culprit since his current theory won't hold water," said Sage.

"I'm afraid he'll just look for a better method of disposal instead of another suspect. In any case this might give us a little more time."

"From the tone of the questioning today, the media isn't interested in embarrassing Burke."

"I expected that from the locals. No matter how they report it, the public will know it happened. They'll know about it if Burke tries to use that theory in court. No matter how it's painted, it's not a viable theory. He'll have to look for a replacement."

"How about the boat theory?"

"It's subject to the same muck problems. The boat can't get close enough and the murderer would have to trek through the same stuff as the horses carrying the victim."

Sage helped the stiff Hack down before heading back to Cocoa Beach.

Snapper was pacing his condo as if it were a cage when Sage returned. The old rancher demanded a blow-by-blow description of the confrontation between his attorney and the media. He derived momentary amusement over the coffee spill, but he was more interested in the questions and answers. He didn't want to wait for the evening news to see the interview.

Sage gave a running commentary on the event, leaving out the personal exchange between him and his attorney.

"I'll bet the whole episode will do nothing to change Burke's mind."

"Actually, I don't think that was the object of the exercise. Hack was more interested in setting up a defense. One of Burke's theories has now been exposed as wanting. Hack is viewing this from a legalistic point of view.

"I happen to view it from another perspective. I believe Burke is an unstable personality. He's using you to be able to stand taller. If he could bring down a legend and appear to solve a heinous crime, he probably feels he can then walk with the big boys. It really doesn't matter if you killed those guys or not. He probably passes you off as being so old that you'll just die before you could cause any appeal problem."

"You have an ugly take on mankind," said Snapper.

"I'm not painting all mankind with this brush....just male snippets like Burke."

Snapper had to go to the bank. Sage decided to have lunch out before changing into his painting clothes. After a quickly eaten sub, Sage headed back for the condo. Golem's van was parked along A-1-A, which made it a pretty good bet he was at the Beach Shanty. Golem was seated with Arty in the back of the bar. Golem waived Sage over.

"What are you doing here on the beach in the middle of a working day?" said Sage as he shook hands with the young deputy states attorney.

"The boss is in such a towering rage that I evacuated. If anyone bitches about it, I'll take sick-time. I'm not going to listen to all that crap, nor am I going to do any of those inane little jobs he's concocting."

"What set him off this time?" said Sage.

"He caught the noon news that covered the interview with Hack. Incidentally, Burke didn't like you before and after he saw you protecting Hack's right flank, you became public enemy number three."

"Three?"

"Yeah, behind Snapper and Hack."

"Oh, boy."

Golem laughed. "I think that, too. Great move with that mug of coffee. Anyone who didn't know you would think it was an accident."

"Yeah, Burke has a Tivo hookup in his office so he can take second looks at items of interest. In your case he watched that coffee incident three times before loudly declaring, "That bastard did that on purpose." As it so happens, that reporterette is one of Burke's admirers. She'd probably have given Hack a bad time."

"Did his little stomp in the swamp change his mind at all?" asked Sage.

"I can't discuss the case, but he ordered a complete set of aerial stereos of the Circle K," said Arty with a grin.

"Then he's just looking for another route," said Sage.

Arty gave a wan little smile, but said nothing.

Chapter 10

—⚏—

As Sage was drinking beer in Cocoa Beach, Snapper was in his bank in Kissimmee removing his name from the ranch accounts, since he had turned the entire operation and land over to Clay. Snapper was acutely aware a new age had begun. Before long the great old ranch would be dissected into itty-bitty plots. Not many years ago such a fate would have been unthinkable.

Snapper was not in the best of moods as he started out of the bank, and he almost ran over Dave Burke. Both men initially started to apologize until they recognized one another.

Burke's mouth snapped shut as he jogged right while Snapper was jogging left leaving them front-to-front again. Even Snapper towered over the diminutive attorney.

A smile broke out on Snapper's face as he looked down on the crown of Burke's hair. "Well. If it isn't our teensy-weensy states attorney in the unretouched flesh."

Burke's darkly tanned skin turned a shade lighter along the jaw line as he snarled back, low enough that only Snapper could hear, "You bastard. I'm going to nail you yet."

"Oh, so I'm a bastard and you're going to nail me yet," said Snapper in a voice loud enough to carry through the Friday afternoon crowd. "I'm glad you ran into me," continued Snapper, as he made a show of rubbing his navel. "Since I no longer own the Circle K, will Arnold Hampton, the developer, have enough use for you to let you continue riding his ticket at the Arendale Country Club?"

Burke's wide eyes swept the banking lobby to see who had heard. "Shut up, you bastard," he hissed. "You'll pay for this." His rage was building. His whole body began to develop tremors.

"You say you'll make me pay for this. How? You may have your suits tailor-made but you still have to buy your jeans in the boys' department."

Burke started to say something but thought better of it. Snapper would just repeat it. He was shaking violently. His fists were clenched.

The two men were still front-to-front. Snapper suddenly bent forward and sniffed loudly. Burke jumped back colliding with the door.

"You may dress like a man," said Snapper in a theatrical whisper, "but there's something missing." Snapper sniffed again. "Now I know what's missing. Why don't we step out back so I can piss on you so you too can smell like a man?"

An older, uniformed security guard had been standing in the background, but when Burke let out an anguished wail, he stepped forward. Burke saw the uniform in his peripheral vision.

"Officer," screamed Burke. "Arrest this bastard."

"I'm security, not that kind of officer," said the old man.

"I said arrest this man. I'm the States Attorney," yelled Burke as he turned his venomous attention to the non-complying officer. When Burke realized who he was talking to, he snarled, "Get a real cop here."

The bank's customer service lady had already started to dial the police to report a disturbance. Other bank patrons were cowering in a corner as Burke started his tirade.

Burke suddenly realized that they were in a public place with numerous witnesses to his outburst. He may have been provoked, but it had been a major political faux pas to have lost control in front of so many voters. With difficulty he regained a modicum of decorum. He acknowledged the phone call that had been placed.

Snapper smiled benignly and took a seat at the customer service desk leaving Burke standing in front of the door. An elderly couple obviously wanted to leave, so Burke moved to the side and tried to look nonchalant as he waited for a patrol car.

There must have been a car in the immediate vicinity, for one appeared almost immediately. The officer hastened into the bank. Burke pointed at Snapper reclining in the bank chair, "Arrest that man." Burke was beginning to get shrill again.

"On what charge, sir?"

"Murder."

"Murder? Is there a body or a warrant?"

"There will be a warrant as soon as I can get back to the office," said Burke in a low voice. He couldn't back down after all his ill-advised blustering.

From his chair a few feet away, Snapper injected, "He's not going to arrest anyone because you had a temper tantrum. You should know that."

"Shut up," snapped Burke. Turning back to the police officer, "You'll be covered."

"I don't want to be covered. I want to be legal. Sorry, Mr. Burke. I need a body and probable cause or a valid warrant. I can't make an arrest on credit. You'd have my hide if I did that on my own. I'll call the chief to make sure, if you'd like."

"Forget the chief. I can wait until tomorrow." The States Attorney pushed his way through the door heading for his car.

The officer turned to Snapper and the customer service lady standing right behind him. "What was that all about?"

"I guess I didn't show him enough respect," said Snapper. "When that happens he can get a little irrational. Thanks for not making it worse. But to protect yourself, you'd better file a report."

The cop nodded his head and withdrew. Snapper turned his chair back toward the Customer Service lady. "Well, Natasha, it looks as if our work isn't done. Under the circumstances I think I need some pocket money. Will you arrange for a $100,000 withdrawal? If you need to borrow on any of my accounts to make that figure, please do so. I'll give you a list on how to distribute the money as soon as you can get it."

A while later Snapper walked out of the bank with a satchel full of small bills. His first stop was a large grocery store where he made a show of stocking up on an abnormally large supply of non-perishable foodstuffs. Then he headed for the ranch while it was still light, waving and honking at locals as he drove by.

At the ranch he became a perpetual motion machine, collecting items that went into the Jeep. In several obscure places around the ranch he made food stashes. He intentionally left the grocery cash register receipt for the food in a plastic bag that was placed under the kitchen work table. Snapper collected pots and pans, leaving vacant spots. A couple of large water jugs were tossed into the Jeep. A note to Golem was slipped under the door to his studio saying, "Keep the house safe from tigers."

After dark, Snapper closed the door to the house without locking it. No sense inviting the authorities to ruin a perfectly good antique door. Snapper took another route off the ranch to avoid anyone who might be watching the normal entrance. Instead of his normal trek into Cocoa, he turned south toward Melbourne, ultimately wending his way across the Indian River onto Merritt Island where he turned north. He drove slowly until he spotted a mailbox almost hidden in the brush next to a narrow track into the trees.

The inauspicious entry belied the residence that stood on the riverbank beyond a good-sized pond. Snapper pulled up to the double garage door. Leaving the lights on, he located the hidden key. Before long, the Jeep was tucked away in a completely enclosed garage beside an older Lexus. Five minutes later Snapper had a bourbon and water sitting at hand while he went through the homeowner's Rolodex. When he found the Cape Cod number he put in a call from one of Arn Ruck's houses to another of Ruck's houses.

"Hey, Arn, This is Snapper. I'm sitting in your Merritt Island place drinking your bourbon. This city water is brutal. I should have brought some spring water."

"You have a mad husband on your trail?" said Arn with a laugh at the thought.

"That would be more fun than my current predicament. Have you heard of that cemetery that they found on my place?"

"Yeah, that news even made it up here when it was found. Haven't heard much about it after the first flurry. What's up?"

"SA Burke can't find anyone else to accuse so he wants to drop that turd into my pocket. We got into it this afternoon in the bank, so I figured I'd better disappear for a bit."

"That Burke is an idiot. It's a good idea to stay out of his way," said Arn. "Make yourself at home. We're not going to be down until the snow flies."

"I don't want to get you involved in this. In case anyone asks, just say it was a standing offer for me to use the place anytime I wanted."

Next, Snapper called information for Tinna Gunn's number and put a call in to her.

"Tinna?"

"Yes."

"This is Snapper Keel from Florida....."

"What has that Cabrone done? Did he hurt himself again?"

"Oh, nothing like that. He's fine. I called to see if you would help me?"

"I suppose so. What do you have in mind?"

"You know about those graves they found on my place?"

"Yes."

"The authorities think I killed those guys. I'm ducking out of sight until things get straightened out. I don't want to get Sage into trouble by calling him. Also they might be able to trace me if I call him directly. So, would you pass my messages along to him?"

"I could do that," said Tinna with poorly concealed eagerness. What Snapper didn't realize was that Tinna had a boundless curiosity and by passing messages along she'd be in the loop.

"I need to let Sage know a couple of things. First, I'm going to send to you the remainder of his fee for the painting. I want the work finished. No matter what happens to me, Sage will have his fee. Second, please ask Sage to collect my mail and have Golem get it to my attorney, Hack, who will take care of bills and any problems that arise. Oh, yes, have Sage tell Golem to continue to use the ranch studio and keep an eye on things."

"I can do that," said Tinna.

"Take down this number." Snapper read off a series of numbers. "That's my cell phone. If Sage has to get in touch with me, have him call you and you call me."

After some small talk, Tinna hung up and armed with an excuse, she called Sage on his cell phone.

"It's past my martini time," declared Tinna when Sage answered.

"Shucks. How long will it take for you to get here?"

"Pendejo. I just had a call from your boss. It sounds as if he's hiding out somewhere. He wants me to be between you two."

"Between us?"

"Yeah. He calls me and I call you. Or you call me and I call him."

"Oh, you're going to be our communication center. The word is 'go-between'."

Whatever." Tinna faithfully relayed Snapper's comments before she let her active imagination start wandering. "What happened to cause him to go hide?"

"Haven't the foggiest idea. I haven't heard of anything happening."

"Do you have a message for Snapper?"

"Not right now. I'll have to check around."

When Tinna rang off, Sage turned the TV on to the Orlando channels to see if there was any news of interest. Nothing. He called Golem and got the answering machine. Sage left a request for a return call. His concentration was broken, so he cleaned up and headed for the beach, where he found Golem's van in the vicinity of the Beach Shanty. However, there was no Golem in the Shanty. The bartender recognized Sage and jerked his head toward the club across the street. "A client's buying him dinner."

Sage dropped onto a stool. He wouldn't interfere with business, but he would have a beer before going home. As he was finishing his longneck, Golem came in the door with his big lopsided grin.

"Figured you were here. Saw Dreadnought."

Sage picked up a couple more beers and led the way to their favorite back table. "Is that smile because I'm here or did you put together another deal?"

"Both," said Golem, diplomatically. "I'm always pleased to see you. You tend to make life interesting. Also I sold three pieces, which are to be installed around a Fiji style pool house. I'm making inroads into the tiki world, which pleases me but will really piss off some local carvers."

"Remember me talking about my tenant potter, Tinna?"

"Who could forget that animated description?"

"She called me a little earlier saying Snapper had called her. He apparently has gone into hiding and he asked her to be the go-between with you and me and Snapper. Have you heard of anything happening? Did Burke issue a warrant?"

"All's been quiet as far as I know."

"Maybe the late news will have something."

"Burke hasn't taken the case to the grand jury. Arty would have known. There was no warrant as of this morning. Let me check around. Are you staying at the condo?"

"Oh, Snapper specifically told Tinna to pass the word for you to continue to use the ranch studio and keep an eye on things."

"Great. I'll be back with you if I can find out anything."

Sage watched the 10:00 o'clock news. There was nothing pertaining to the Keel case. Sage fussed around his painting just doing busywork. He was in no mood to be creative with paint. His mind was going at supersonic speeds on other considerations.

There was nothing on any of the news channels. Golem didn't call. Sage finally retreated to bed where he tossed and turned. He couldn't shut off his mind. He was more convinced than ever that Snapper had to know the murderer. It seemed inconceivable that someone could be trespassing for decades on Keel land and not come to Snapper's attention. From Sage's knowledge of ranch life, he could not imagine Burke's scenario of Snapper bringing victims back to a working ranch to have his fun. With all those people always around, how could he have transported the bodies to the burial site, even at night? It just didn't fit. It defied logic. Apparently logic couldn't compete for consideration alongside a picture of a fancy shotgun and string of birds. Sage had been trying to figure out a way of jogging Snapper's memory, but now that Snapper had gone to ground, that wasn't going to work.

Chapter 11

—ɯɯ—

The tiff at the bank did not become common knowledge, so there were no ripples on the water the next morning. Sage checked with Mona and found that the condo was still being watched. Golem dropped by at his regular painting viewing time with no information. "I called Arty but got his voice mail. He hasn't returned my call," said Golem. "Of course, there is no way of knowing. He might be ducking my call, but I usually get a call-back."

"Something sent Snapper into a hole. I'll call Hack and see if he knows anything."

From the sound of the coffee roaster in the background, Sage figured that Hack was in the Cowhunter Saloon. "Hack, this is Sage. Have you recovered enough to go line-dancing?"

"I'll never recover that much. What's on your mind?"

"Have you heard anything that might cause Snapper to go to ground?"

"Are you at the condo?"

"Yes."

"Why don't you take a walk out onto the patio and give me a call on your cell?" Hack hung up.

"Something must have happened. Hack didn't want to talk on this phone. Grab your coffee and let's get some air."

Sage and Golem settled at a patio table behind the hurricane shutter Sage had lowered to irritate the prying eyes. Sage redialed Hack.

The first thing the attorney wanted to know was why Sage was asking about Snapper.

"I received a call from my Albuquerque associate saying Snapper had asked her to be a go-between for him and me and others. He asked Golem to take his mail to you. He is sending the balance of my bill for the painting to her. He also wants Golem to continue to use his sculpture studio at the ranch and watch over things. He said he was ducking out of sight until things clear up. I was trying to find out what precipitated that action."

"Just a little bit ago I was told Snapper and Burke came nose-to-nose, so to speak, in the bank. Snapper seriously questioned Burke's manhood any number of times in public. Burke lost it and tried to have Snapper arrested without a warrant. I would imagine Burke is trying to get that warrant now. I'll call around and let you know. If Burke gets a warrant it will be on his own hook. The grand jury is not in session now. Don't use that condo phone for anything important. Burke may have it tapped if he can't find our friend." The phone went dead.

Sage passed the instructions on to Golem. Since there wasn't enough information to any more than guess, Sage and Golem returned to their respective projects.

The lead story on the evening news was that States Attorney Burke had issued a warrant for the arrest of local legend Snapper Keel for the 1948 murder of a young male.

Golem must have heard the same announcement because his name appeared on the Caller ID.

"You watching TV?"

"Yeah."

"Buy you a beer at the Shanty."

"That's the best offer I've had in a long time. Be there as soon as I can put my paints away."

Golem's van was parked on the street when Sage got there. He and Arty Misconi were seated as their usual back table. Sage stepped over a chair back and sat down. His Coors was already there.

"Hey, Arty," said Sage. "You're a long ways from home on a weekday....again."

"I'm hiding....again. One of these days I must buy a new phone battery...one that holds its charge."

"What is it this time?"

"Same thing. The boss has had a tantrum relapse. He's been hand-carrying the paper work that is needed for Keel's murder warrant from office to office. When there's going to be some delay, he rushes back to his office to sort pictures."

"Sort pictures?"

"Remember me telling you about that Polaroid picture cube and the Monday morning changing routine?"

Sage and Golem both nodded.

He's going through those hundreds of photos picking out all shots with him wearing jeans."

"Wearing jeans?" said Golem.

"In that bank confrontation, Snapper announced to the world that Burke bought his jeans in the boy's department. Burke called for a shredder to be moved into his office. He ran a few of the photos through the machine. It cut the paper into strips. He had the first shredder replaced with one that also crosscuts to make confetti."

Golem rolled his eyes toward the ceiling. Sage frowned before saying, "That sounds a little excessive to me."

Arty shrugged. "I think the excessive thing is pushing for a warrant. We don't have a case built....but you never heard that from me."

"What else happened at that dust off?" said Sage.

"There are all sorts of versions, but as close as I can figure it, Snapper said that since he no longer owned the ranch, would the developer still let him go to the golf club. Snapper also offered to piss on him so he could smell like a man."

It was Sage's turn to inspect the flyspecks over his head. "With an oversensitive diminutive male who has a modicum of power, I think I'd find a hole too. Snapper should know what kind of reaction there would be. He must have wanted Burke to seek a warrant."

"Snapper was never noted for putting up with incompetence or stupidity," said Golem. "Burke's antics may have been wearing on Snapper's patience."

"By forcing a warrant to be issued, Snapper may have to sit in jail for a long time. But this will force Burke to present his case in a preliminary hearing where the defense will hear what it's facing. With the grand jury, Burke's case would still be hidden."

Golem had his face screwed into a frown. "Someone once said Burke didn't have a case yet. What will happen when he has to have a preliminary hearing?"

"He doesn't have to try the case. All he has to show is that probably a crime was committed and probably Snapper committed it. He can prove there was a crime but the second part is tricky. He can't just say that the grave is on someone's property, so he must have done it, because I can't find another suspect. There will have to be something more."

"What happens if they can't find Snapper?" said Sage.

"If after turning over all the local rocks, they can't find him, Burke will probably go for a fugitive warrant to expand the search."

"When will he have the warrant?" asked Sage.

"Probably he has it now," said Arty. That's one of the reasons I'm hiding. Burke's already squandered a good portion of his budget with surveillance and special scientific lab work. He's working the tail off everyone, without pay, on useless chores designed to make it look as if we're understaffed and underfunded. The Keel investigation gives him a cause célèbre with which to make political hay."

"He sounds like a strange boss," said Sage.

Arty shrugged. "That would take a value judgment. I deal in facts, not in speculation. You'll have to draw your own conclusions."

"In any case," said Golem, to change the subject, "I wonder if Snapper knows about the warrant."

"He probably foresaw it as a result of that meeting in the bank," said Sage. "I'm pretty sure that it wasn't planned. Snapper went in for a rather long session over the ranch transfer. I would think it was a chance meeting, but a well thought-out confrontation on Snapper's part....and he probably understood the ramifications of the jibes."

"Then you think he knows they're looking for him," said Golem.

"Depends on where he is." Sage took another swig. "If he's on the ranch he wouldn't have access to the news unless he uses the Jeep radio."

"He wasn't at the old ranch house this morning when I was there," said Golem.

Sage held his bottle up and made a circular motion to the bartender to order another round. "The next time you're at the condo, look at the aerial photos on the wall of Snapper's bedroom. That ranch is composed of many old landholdings. There are hundreds of abandoned buildings scattered over the Circle K. Some of them have been used for storage or shelters for the hands while working the ranch. He could be camped anywhere."

Arty sighed. "Tomorrow, Burke will call out of the troops and the hunt will be on. The law enforcement agencies will be actively looking and everyone else will be pulling surveillance."

"If you're assigned to the condo behind Snapper's place, come on over for a beer. It's more comfortable there."

Arty flushed a little bit. "You know about that."

"Yeah, that and up by the owl on the roof."

"How'd you spot 'em?"

"Snapper picked them up immediately," said Sage. "I'd better get back to my work. It's only now that I feel like I'm regaining my dexterity."

When Sage arrived at the condo, he put in a call to Tinna. "Have you heard anything from our friend?"

"No."

After catching up on the home news and massaging Tinna's libido a bit, he asked her to call Snapper to report the issuance of a warrant for him.

Half an hour later a call came from New Mexico. Tinna reported, "He's not answering his phone. I've tried every ten minutes. I'll continue trying until I go to bed. I'll give you a call when I get through."

That negative contact started a very long, nervous week as the local media featured the manhunt as their lead story.

The day after the conversation with Arty, Golem showed up at the condo at noon. That was the first time Sage had ever seen the carver mad, and when Golem got mad, he was mad all over. He shuffled his feet, twitched and moved his long, lank torso in various contortions. His eye shadow was even larger and darker.

"I went to the ranch to work. Those dirty-assed bastards wouldn't let me in."

"Which dirty-asses?"

"I didn't see anyone around until I crowned over the little hill above the house. I was stopped at gun-point by a member of a swat team. He made me lay face down on the ground while he rifled through my pockets and searched my van. The place was swarming with deputies.

"He made me lie there for fifteen or twenty minutes while others went into buildings. My studio was standing wide open. They had to go through a lock to get in. I watched them cut off locks on several of the outbuildings. From my position on the ground I could see under the van. I watched the whole thing.

"When I tried to ask what was going on, that Neanderthal in a flak jacket told me to shut up as he nudged me with a boot. When I demanded to see a search warrant to break into my studio, that low-life hooked my nostril with the front sight on his automatic weapon and jerked my head around so he could sneer in my face. He said, "Not another peep out of you, Loony, if you know what's good for you."

"Did he hurt you?"

"He nicked the inside of my nose, but nothing else. There were four of them going through the ranch house. I didn't see them take anything out of there, but there was quite a commotion around one of the outbuildings. They took what looked like four plastic grocery sacks away."

"Do you think they were looking for Snapper, or have they found him and they were looking for evidence?"

"Oh, I don't think they've found Snapper. They may have been looking for an indication of where he might be, but they weren't searching for murder evidence. They were searching places big enough to hide a man and they were covering each other as if they expected to be shot at."

"It would have surprised me if Snapper could have been found that easily."

"They must think he's out on the ranch. Most of the cars didn't come out. They fanned out cross-country.

"There's probably going to be a bunch of stuck cars out there."

"A car stopped by to pick up that bastard that was guarding me. He didn't say a word before leaving. And he took my van keys with him or threw them into the bushes. It's lucky I had a hidden key. That guy is really on my shit list."

"When everyone left, I checked my studio. Nothing much was disturbed. The lock had been cut off. Apparently, Snapper had left the house unlocked. They went through most everything in the house. Before I left, I closed all the buildings. Then I came here. I was too mad to carve. All that would have come out is gargoyles."

"Let's go out for some lunch," said Sage as he made a telephoning motion to Golem.

Before they went into the restaurant, Sage used a pay phone

to call Hack. The attorney wasn't answering his cell, so Sage left a message on his voice mail reporting the search of the ranch. He also said that their friend was still out of touch.

Then Sage called Tinna to give her the info concerning the search in case Snapper checked in.

During the next week Mona Hatfield reported that the watchers were back but in another unit. Golem knew the ranch was under surveillance because when the wind was coming from the right direction he could smell cigarette smoke.

Clay Keel called Sage, apparently figuring that when his grandfather surfaced, he'd probably get in touch with Sage. Clay said he'd just been to the County Commissioners office to put in a formal bitch that the personnel of the Sheriffs Office and the States Attorneys Office had been abusing the search warrant that had been issued to look for Snapper on the ranch. He said the county could expect a sizeable bill for damages. Searchers were cutting fences, leaving gates open, damaging pasture, damaging buildings, causing injury to livestock and giving ranch hands a bad time. He said he had flown over the ranch and it looked like a plate of spaghetti with all the tire tracks running through the pastures. All that traffic was running weight off his livestock.

Since Sage was talking on the condo phone, he told Clay, "I haven't heard a peep from Snapper. It seems they still think he's hiding on the ranch. Have they found the Jeep yet?"

"No. Of course, there are hundreds of hiding places. The police have staked out mom's and my place in case granddad shows up. They're wasting their time. They'll never catch that old fox that way. If they had any sense of humor or professional pride, he'd probably take those stakeouts down, hog tie them and leave them for the next shift. But, today they'd just scream felonious assault."

Sage was well into the painting. The details were getting finer and finer. He was beginning to worry that he'd finish his work and the big mystery would still be unsolved. He'd been away from the Hacienda too long, which always caused no little distress, but he was finding it more disturbing to think of walking out on a mystery in which he had such an involvement. And he was looking forward to a payback time with the bomber.

In an effort to extend his stay in Florida, Sage cut back on brush-time. He started meeting Golem for a beer at the Beach Shanty in the evenings. Then they'd go out for dinner. He let Golem select the places in keeping with the carver's economic status. There was an amazing assortment of savory entrées to be found in the most unusual places. Sage enjoyed his tour of the local eateries.

Of course, the main topic of conversation was Snapper's situation. One night Golem said, "I found out why they keep sniffing around the ranch."

"Why?"

"When they pulled that first search of the ranch house, they found a long supermarket cash register tape for a ton of staple, camp-style food and supplies. They think they found part of his stash in that outbuilding where I watched the deputies carry away those grocery bags."

"One would think that by now they could have covered everything a dozen times."

"According to Arty, the guys in the field have been having a hard time convincing Burke that Snapper's not there. Burke has reluctantly agreed to expand the search into other jurisdictions. He really wants to be in on the 'kill,' so to speak."

"Well, one good thing is that since Snapper is missing, the real murderer hasn't been around creating mischief."

"What do you supposed happened to Snapper's cell phone?"

"No telling," said Sage. "As unfamiliar as Snapper is with new nerdy things, he may have turned it off and can't get it on again. The battery may have gone out or he simply lost it. In any case, he can't just run out to a service center or store. When he wants to get in touch with someone, he'll find a way."

"Tomorrow I'm going to the ranch to start half a dozen new pieces. I'm about to run out of palm logs. I wish the authorities would move out. If I'd go out to cut palms, I'd have a dozen deputies on my trail thinking I'm going to make contact with Snapper.

"But, the first thing I have to do is find a dead rat or small animal that's stinking up my studio."

The next evening Golem was a little late in getting to the Beach Shanty. Sage greeted him with, "How was your rat hunt?"

"Didn't find it, and it's something bigger than a rat. It smells up the whole area. I'm figuring maybe it's an alligator or cow that's stuck in the weeds in the lake. I'll take the johnboat out to see if I can find it and tow it away. It's getting pretty ripe."

"Have you seen the local papers?"

"No," said Golem. "What's happening?"

"Burke gave another press conference where he asked the public to help find Snapper. There were some poor, old photos. Apparently, Snapper is a little camera shy."

"It's probably more like the people who have recent pictures wouldn't let Burke use them. Not too many people that I've talked to think Snapper would ever do such a thing. Burke's not getting much public support in Osceola County."

"How's his political base?"

Golem shrugged. "The base is good. Burke was elected because of party affiliation instead of experience or ability. Since he was running against another unknown, he had an easy time of it. This time it's a little different. He will have a record to run on and if it's bad it can be used against him. That's why he's so sensitive about his public image."

After a swig of beer, Sage said, "I wish Snapper would check in. I need for him to give me a date for that view of the room."

"Why?"

"I'm lettering the names and heights of all the Keel kids on the back door. If this is a view from fifty years ago, I shouldn't include Clay's height. On the other hand, he may want to include important elements independent of age. We never talked about that."

"Don't come down here for the next couple of days, unless I call," said Golem. "I have a bunch of installations stacked up. You can never tell how long one will take. I'll be done when I'm done."

Sage stayed at the condo for the next couple of days putting in smaller and smaller details. He was making work. Normally, he raced down the home stretch on a painting so he could turn Dreadnought's radiator cap in Albuquerque's direction and make best time back to the Hacienda. But this time there were too many items of unfinished business. He could claim a personal stake in the events because of the broken arm.

On the third morning, Golem called. He was noticeably upset. "Sage, I've just been out at the ranch. That odor is really bad. And I'm getting a bad feeling about it. I've been around decomposing animals before but this odor is different. I've never been around a dead person. I hear that is a smell all its own. I hate to do this to you but could you come out here and help me find the source?"

"I'll be there in an hour."

"I'll meet you at the entry to the ranch."

Because of the flatness of the land, Golem's van was easy to spot from a considerable distance. The carver was leaning against the shadow side of the box. He came over and kneeled down so he could see into Dreadnought.

"Don't like being such a wimp. You know Snapper has been missing for weeks. I got to thinking about that as I was driving in this morning and then the stench. Everything was ganging up on me, so I drove out and called you."

"Don't worry about it. I'll follow you in."

"Park your car by the bridge that blew up. No sense in stinking up Dreadnought. You'll be able to smell it in the van."

At the bridge, Sage crawled into the van and wrinkled his nose. "Can you tell where the smell is the worst?"

Golem pulled up next to his studio. The odor was quite intense. "It seems to lie in a cloud over the whole area. The slight movement of air wasn't any help finding the source. Sage, with Golem tagging behind, moved slowly toward the big barn and the lake beyond. The pair walked out on the dock. The gentle flowing air from the cooler lake water to the faster warming land was noticeably less pungent.

"I think the source is going to be on the land," said Sage as he headed back through the outbuildings toward the house. Sage stopped abruptly and Golem nearly ran over him.

"What....?"

"Sh...." hissed Sage. "Listen."

Golem cocked his head to concentrate. After a bit he said, "What?"

"Flies. That way." Sage started to move through a cluster of outbuildings.

Sage stopped and pointed. "There." He was indicating a small tool shed. Big, black flies were swarming around the open eaves.

Leading the way, Sage circled around another shed to get to the front of the suspect building, so they could see the door. There was a brass lock in the hasp.

"After all the searchers left, I checked all these building. None of them were locked. The ones that were normally locked were broken into by the deputies. All the buildings have locks, but they were either over the door or on a nail inside. Someone has locked this since I made the rounds."

"Know where the keys are?"

"No, but there are bolt cutters in the big tool shed."

"Get one."

Golem moved off. Sage watched the flies move in and out of the cracks. The odor was intense.

When Golem returned, Sage took a breath and headed for the door. He easily cut the small brass lock, quickly unfastened the hasp and flung the door open. A great cloud of flies and stench boiled out the door.

Gagging, Sage quickly retreated to join Golem. After he caught his breath, he turned to look at the building expecting to see a body. Instead here was a powder blue object lying in a clear space just inside the door.

Sage took a deep breath of the lesser fouled air and returned for a closer look. Golem stayed where he was. The object was a light blue blanket tied with binding twine. There was obviously a body inside.

From the description he had heard, the blue bundle appeared to be a new victim of the graveyard murderer.

Sage retreated back toward the house, jerking his head for Golem to follow. After taking a moment to try calming his jumpy stomach, Sage said, "I think this is victim number 21."

"Could it be Snapper? He's been gone a long time."

"Don't know. If it isn't, it's still not good for Snapper. Burke will be certain that he's named the right man."

"What are we going to do?"

"Take me back to my car. I'll make a call to the sheriff's office from there and I'll pick up my camera."

Sage called information for the sheriff's number and called directly, asking for Tony Lopez. He had to give his name to get through.

"Hi Sage, what's up?"

"Golem and I are at Keel's old ranch house. We were trying to locate the source of a nasty odor. We found it. It's a blanket-wrapped bundle tied in binding twine."

"Oh, boy."

"We'll be waiting at the blown out bridge. Be warned, it's really stinky out here."

"I'll be out of here in five minutes. The forensic boys will be right behind."

"How about not telling the SA until you find out what you've got."

"Good idea. I'll see you in a bit."

As Sage dug out his Elph, he said to Golem, "I'm going to get some pictures."

"Unless you need some help, I'll just stay here."

"This is a one-man job. See ya shortly."

Sage headed back over the knoll. He started taking pictures at the house to demonstrate locality. When he got to the shed, he held his breath to move in close enough to take close-ups of the body and the shed. He also took photos of the ground around the building as well as some shoe and tire tracks on the nearby roadway.

Sage went back to the vehicles. He tucked the Elph into one of Dreadnought's hidey-holes. Tony wasn't there yet. He wouldn't be running under red light and siren because the victim wasn't going anywhere.

Golem was looking better. He asked again, "You don't think that's Snapper?"

"It could be, but I doubt it. If it is, that could raise hell with Burke's case."

"Yeah," said Golem with a grimace. "If it's not, Burke will have the ranch turned upside down again looking for him."

"If that body is another young male, it's going to convert a lot of people to Burke's line of thinking. However, as far as I am concerned, it furthers my argument that the killer has a long-standing familiarity with the ranch."

"Like who?"

"A former employee, the vet who used to come out to tend sick critters, the driver of the petroleum truck that delivered gas, diesel, oil or whatever products they used on the ranch. Over the decades there probably have been hundreds."

"I think Tony is coming. At least a fast-moving dust cloud is approaching."

Tony slowed down so he wouldn't drag a cloud of dust over the meeting spot. Lopez and another detective climbed out of the car. Tony greeted the artists with, "If you've got another body, that's not going to help your friend's case. Where is it?"

Sage could see Golem wasn't at all keen about going back in, so he said, "Golem, how about hanging around out here and directing the forensic boys in?"

Golem didn't let his appreciation show as he said, "All right, I'll do that."

Sage climbed into the back of the unmarked patrol car, preferring to save the effort of cleaning Dreadnought. "Go past the house toward the barn. The shed is in the second row of buildings on the left. However, you might find it preferable to park by the house and walk in."

"That bad, huh?"

"It is to me, but this isn't my area of expertise."

"I hear this is a small find for you."

"Someone has been talking when he should have been listening," said Sage sourly.

"Someone ran your name on the internet. You take up a lot of space on Google. That was intriguing enough for the guys to take up a collection to buy your ebook. The sheriff doesn't know it, but his budget financed the printing. It's making the rounds now. I get it next."

"Those bodies weren't this fresh."

"I smell your point," said Tony as he tested the air after parking the car.

Sage elected to remain at a distance. "There was a brass lock that we cut off with bolt cutters. The lock and hasp will probably have my prints on them. Golem checked all the building after you guys finally left. This shed was not locked at that time."

The two detectives took a quick look at the setup and retreated to their car. "We'll let the techies handle that part of the investigation. How'd you happen to find the body?"

"The whole thing started with Golem noting a bad smell. Let's go back to the bridge so he can fill in the background."

Golem started the story and Sage finished up. They were through with their account before the forensic squad arrived leading a meat-wagon to remove the body.

Tony went to talk with the squad leader. He found out that the bundle would not be opened until it was in the lab. "There's no sense in hanging around here. We won't learn anything about the contents until tomorrow at the earliest. I'll call some patrolmen in to guard the scene. I'll give you a call tomorrow to let you know if it's Snapper or not."

On the way back home Sage stopped at one of the few pay phones to survive the cell phone craze to put in a call to Tinna. Surprisingly she was at her apartment.

"Hi, what are you doing home at this hour? I figured I'd be talking to your machine."

"I'm unloading another truck load of those Mexican animal pots. Do you realize that the first batch is either sold or on order?"

"Congratulations. How is the Hacienda?"

"Outside of an armadillo living under the tool shed, everything's fine. When are you coming home?"

"The painting is pretty much finished but with Snapper gone, I can't get an approval on it." Sage proceeded to tell Tinna what had just transpired. "If Snapper checks in, tell him I need to talk with him before he does anything."

Sage went on to the condo, where he stripped to the skin, dumped his clothes into the washer and set the heavy wash cycle.

He spent a longer period than normal in the shower trying to cleanse both body and mind.

It proved to be a long day and night. The next morning Golem came to share the vigil. The finding of the body was the lead story on both the Orlando news stations and Florida Today and Orlando Sentinel newspapers. There was no news on the contents of the bundle but the sheriff and states attorney promised a press conference as soon as the contents had been examined.

It was lunchtime before Tony called. "I'm calling from a friend's phone. Under the circumstances I don't want your number on my phone records. The body is not Snapper's. We should be able to identify it because prints are available as well as a fair physical description. That's about all I can say. Keep your heads down. Burke is having a screaming fit because the sheriff wasn't able to find the killer before he was able to kill again. Burke is going berserk. And he is not making any points by calling the sheriff and his whole staff incompetent boobs. Tell Golem it wouldn't be wise to go to his studio right now." Tony didn't wait around for any questions.

At 2:00 pm there was the promised press conference from the

Osceola Court House. Sheriff Byron Lord was the primary presenter, giving the bare essentials concerning the find. He did not identify Sage and Golem by name but referred to them as legal invitees to the property. He stated that the time of death was still undetermined, but that indications were that death had occurred about two weeks earlier. The only identification of the remains was that the body appeared to be that of a young adult male. Further identification was waiting on fingerprint and possibly DNA comparisons.

The sheriff's presentation was terse and to the point. When reporters started expanding on his remarks he firmly refused to enter into further speculation.

When one reporter shouted over the hubbub, "Is this number twenty-one on Keel's list?" Burke, who had been fidgeting all over the back stage, bounded forward. However, the podium the sheriff had been using was much too high, so he grabbed the mike out of the holder and advanced to the front of the dais.

"That's in my realm. I have issued an arrest warrant for Olin Snapper Keel for a previously discovered body on his ranch. Preliminary investigation tends to indicate that the last killing was perpetrated by the same individual. There are similarities too numerous to ignore that leads us to believe we are dealing with the same perpetrator.

"There were indications that the wanted Keel has gone to ground on his ranch here in Osceola County. However, after an extensive search of that ranch was conducted, my office was assured that Keel was not there. Now we have another victim."

Quick to pick up on the implications, several reporters formed similar questions directed to the sheriff, trying to find out if he believed Keel was still hiding on the ranch.

The sheriff started to reply before he remembered the mike was not on the stand. Burke gave no indication that he was going to relinquish the PA system, so the sheriff projected his bull voice over Burke's head.

"I have no information concerning Keel's whereabouts. Although our investigation has not been able to ascribe culpability to anyone, we will, in accordance with the law, serve Mr. Burke's warrant whenever we locate Mr. Keel."

The sheriff could see the state of the media's feeding frenzy. A spat between two major county officials could spark an event and he wanted no part of it.

The sheriff said, "Thank you for coming," and with solemn dignity, he marched back into the courthouse.

Burke shot the sheriff a murderous glance but held his ground. With resolve, he turned to face the media with its myriad of questions.

Sage and Golem had been taking in the whole scenario over TV at the condo. Neither had much to say. They were lost in their own assessments of how the situation would affect their lives.

"None of this is good for Snapper," said Golem.

"Oh, I don't know. At least we now know the sheriff's investigation hasn't stuck Snapper with the crimes. Burke is the one that's leading the charge."

"That's the woman you doused with coffee," said Golem.

The camera was focused on the female reporter, who was asking, "Is this new discovery going to help your case on Keel?"

The scene shifted back to Burke. "It is too early to tell, but indications are that all the murders were committed by the same person. There may be additional evidence that can be gathered from the fresh victim. My hope is that such evidence will clinch the case."

"Did you get killer DNA from the body?" asked another reporter.

"I'm not at liberty to discuss that," said Burke.

"You have a warrant out for Keel," said a print reporter, "and you haven't found him. If he's your man, then he must still be around here since this new body is the work of the same person. Where do you go from here?"

"I've asked the sheriff for a more exhaustive search of the ranch and I'm making arrangements to bring in new equipment to assist."

Someone yelled, "What kind of equipment?"

Burke smiled. "I'm sure Keel would like to know."

"I still think Burke is after the wrong guy," said Sage. "Until he quits looking for Snapper, he'll never look for anyone else. It appears as if we'll have to remove Burke from the picture."

Golem's head snapped around from the TV. His dark, sunken eyes were wide.

"What?"

"Don't look so shocked. I'm not going to do away with him. I just want to give him a little push over the edge so he has to be replaced. That shouldn't be too hard."

"How do you propose to do that?"

"He's well on his way. That horse ride around the lake got things rolling. Then Snapper's encounter at the bank really set him off. Then this tiff with the sheriff isn't helping his cause. Remember Arty's remark about cutting up the jeans photos?"

"How do you think you can exert pressure on him? You're a foreigner around here."

"I'll have to give it some more thought but for starters, do you know anyone who works in Plexiglas?"

"Yeah, there's a guy down at the port that makes Plexiglass windows for boats. He also does custom fabrications."

"Do you know how those Polaroid cubes work?"

"They're a five sided clear box with a cardboard box inside to hold the pictures in place."

"Right. Could you order a cube just like it but with an interior dimension of 8½ inches? Better make it 8⅝ interior, along with an interior box to hold the pictures in place. Oh yes, have him make some sort of device to hold the thing together so it can be passed around. I'll pay for it."

"What are you going to do with it?"

"I'll show you as soon as I know," said Sage with a wicked grin.

Golem left to go place the order before he was expected elsewhere. Sage headed to a drugstore to make a CD of the images on his

Elph's memory card. He also bought a mailer and sent the copies to Ro, a friend and business partner in San Francisco.

Before leaving the post office parking lot, Sage sat for a while in Dreadnought organizing his thoughts to a classical music background from NPR. Once a plan was in place, he drove to a coffee house for a cup of dark roast to take with him to one of the beach parks.

Sage parked himself on one of the dune crossover rails and pulled Ro's number out of his phone's memory.

"Are you going to make it here by margarita time?" demanded the tiny investigative reporter when she recognized Sage's number on her Caller ID.

"I'm a little too far away. I'm still in Florida."

"You should have already finished there. Are you in jail or something?"

"Or something. I've got a little states attorney here that keeps trying to put my boss in jail. This attorney hates to be staring at my belly button when he is trying to go mano-a-mano with me.

"You could probably go nose-to-nose with him. Anyway, I want to take the case away from him. He's walking on the edge now. A little nudge would topple him. In any case, twenty and now maybe twenty-one mutilated young males could be a tantalizing story and, as far as I can see, it's not getting much coverage beyond the local scene. It may be fertile territory for a little of your style of investigative reporting."

"Tell me more."

Sage ran up a considerable phone bill presenting his case to Ro, who began to show increased interest when Sage gave an account of the new body and the morning press conference.

"I'm getting a little bored with my current project. There's no time limit and a Florida trip might get me into a better mood for the final mind-numbing slog. Give me some names and dates. I'll see what's out there and if there's any room for me."

Sage ran through the names of the principal characters and

pertinent dates.

"That should be enough to start a Nexis search," said Ro.

Sage smiled. He was confident the hook had been set.

"Give me a call and I'll pick you up at the Orlando or Melbourne airport. Since Snapper is among the missing, you can stay in the master suite.   If he comes back you might have to move in with me."

"That would be like old times, wouldn't it?"

When Sage returned to the condo, he rummaged around in his supplies in Dreadnought for drawing pencils and paper. That evening he kept pushing a pencil. He broke long enough to heat a frozen dinner. Before he turned in, he had seven 8½ inch square cartoons depicting Burke in anything but complimentary situations. He jotted down a few more cartoon ideas before retiring.

The drawings were lying on the breakfast table when Golem arrived for coffee. He must have squeezed his friend because he already had a Plexiglas cube.

Golem made the rounds of the cartoons, laughing at each in turn. "I hope you're wearing your Kevlar vest. You've seen how he reacts to trivial slights. These are direct frontal assaults on his size, masculinity, honor and sexual capacity."

"Good. I'd hate to have all that work go for naught. Help me mount five of them in the cube. The other two are replacements. I'd like to be able to change one each day to build a sustained interest."

"Where do you come up with all these ideas?" said Golem as he held up a drawing of a very large, well endowed blonde standing in a provocative stance. A caricature of Burke was standing on tall, platform sneakers reaching up to pluck the blonde's sleeve. The caption read, "I can do that, too."

"The girl is my tenant, Tinna. In any sexual encounter, she'd suck him in and spit out his platform shoes, no matter how much he brags about himself."

"How about the gavel?" The drawing depicted a large gavel lying on the table. A tiny caricature of Burke was sitting spread-legged on the sound block pounding on the block between his legs with a toy hammer and shouting, "This meeting will come to order."

"Just small and ineffectual," said Sage. "Do you want to ride along? I'm going to take this to the Cowhunter Saloon. I'll have to talk the owner into putting it on the bar. If he's not of the right political persuasion, that might be difficult. I'm hoping people will come in each day to check out the new drawing. I think it would be good for business."

"Can Burke give the saloon any grief?"

"I don't think he can legally because he's a public figure. He's fair game. He might harass the establishment and maybe even sic regulators on it. However, if that was ever proven, Burke could be in real trouble."

Sage pulled Dreadnought up to the front window of Cowhunter Saloon. It must have been a slack period. The girl behind the bar was alone because, Naomi, the owner, was on a milk run. She'd be back shortly. Sage and Golem bought coffees and sat at a back table. Before they finished their drinks, an attractive, young women came in, lugging four gallons of milk. After consultation with the gal behind the counter, the owner headed for their table.

She stuck her hand out. "I'm Naomi. I own this joint. My girl tells me you're the one who dumped some of Cowhunter's best down the front of a smart a.....a self-centered reporter." She smiled broadly at the thought. "That little episode was good for business."

"Yeah, I was the clumsy one. This is my friend Golem."

"I see images of you all over the country. What can I do for you?"

"How'd you like to boost your business a little more?" asked Sage.

"I never turn down an opportunity to improve my business."

Sage pulled the Plexiglas cube out of a plastic grocery bag. "Just leave this on the bar for your customers to see." He shoved the cube across the table.

Naomi started laughing as she flipped the cube around to see all the drawings.

` "I can send a replacement a day. They will be numbered so if you have someone remove the lowest number and put in a new one, it would be fresh daily."

"Could I post the old ones on the bulletin board?"

"It would be better for business if you didn't. If you post them, a person could come in once a week to see that week's additions. If you don't post them, anyone who wants to follow the series has to come in daily to keep up."

A female foursome entered the coffee house. They were lined up at the bar waiting for their drinks. Naomi stood up with the cube. "May I?" Without waiting for an answer, she walked to the end of the bar and slid the cube like an experienced barmaid slides a beer down to a patron. "Have you seen these?"

The first woman caught the cube and guffawed before the rest could see anything. A pointing and laughing fest broke out. One said, "Can you take his clothes off?"

"I'll ask," said Naomi.

A couple of men with a traveling chess set came in. They joined the women, who were pointing out the various subtleties that Sage had included.

Naomi returned to the table. "It appears your cube is a hit. What's the catch?"

"No catch. Your states attorney is following a plan of action against a friend. I just want to get under his skin and give him something else to occupy his time. When he gets his thinking straightened out, I'll quit."

"You're not going to try charging me are you?"

"No. Here are two more cartoons. Before I leave, give me your address and I'll send new ones. You'll have to change them."

"That I can do."

A couple of days later, Burke's reference to specialized equipment became the lead news item in the local media. Burke had borrowed a military heat-seeking scanner for an aircraft. The press hailed the new approach until it became evident that the scanner spotted cows even better than people. The operators had hits from every thicket on the property.

As Golem was watching the morning news over his coffee, he said, "Snapper may be out there but why do they think he's on the Circle K? There's a whole lot of vacant territory surrounding Snapper's ranch where he could be hiding. It doesn't seem they are looking beyond the property lines."

"Clay has been screaming his head off to the commissioners about the sheriff disrupting the ranch routine and running weight off his cattle. Burke has a warrant to search the Circle K, but I'll bet he'd have difficulties getting onto other properties, especially those run by corporations."

"It looks as if they're turning over every cow chip," said Golem.

"They won't find him."

"How can you say that?"

"Oh, I don't know, but why would Snapper sit out in the bush for weeks, slapping mosquitoes?....and he'd have run out of bourbon by now. Oh, he could do it if necessary, but why, when you don't have to?"

"All law enforcement agencies are looking for him. His Jeep would be easy to spot."

"With Snapper's money, he could be anywhere, driving anything."

"The cops would surely be watching his bank accounts and credit cards."

"Right, but Snapper knows a lot of people. How long do you suppose it'd be before Jake could slip him $50,000 in untraceable bills?"

"See what you mean."

The telephone rang. The call was from Ro.

"Hey," she said, "I'm flying into Orlando tomorrow morning at 11.40."

"What flight? I'll pick you up."

"No, I'll need a car. Just tell me how to get there."

"Find 528 East. Keep coming to Cocoa Beach. You'll see Ron

Jon's Surf show on the left. Can't miss it. Pass Ron Jon's and take the first street to the right. You'll see Riverwood Condo at the end. When you get here, give me a call and I'll show you where to park."

"Is that the Red Flea you've talked about?" said Golem after Sage hung up.

"Right, but I wouldn't push that moniker. She tolerated it because it gives her notoriety but she really doesn't like it thrown in her face."

"Is she coming for a visit or work?"

"Work. We have a big case that's getting only Burke directed publicity. Ro is a crack investigative reporter. Her presence makes the media a little more cautious on how they handle the news. If she refutes them in a major publication, it's not a career-promoting event. Local media doesn't like looking foolish or stupid on a national scale."

Golem was shirking his duties to be around when Ro arrived. He hung back as Sage headed for the bright red Mustang GT Convertible at the front entry. The door flew open. A great mass of flaming red hair on an itty-bitty female erupted out of the car and flung herself into Sage's arms. She wrapped her arms around the painter's neck and gave him a resounding kiss.

Ro relaxed her grip on Sage's neck so she could slide down his front until she stood on the pavement. Sage was chuckling merrily as he said, "Ro, I'd like you to meet a friend, Golem. Actually, it's Gordon Lemry."

Ro marched straight at Golem until her nose almost touched his naval region. Then she began a slow scan up Golem's frame until she focused on the long, sunken-eyed face. "Boy, they grow tall and straggly in this salt air." Ro stuck out her hand and wrapped a large, warm smile on her face. "Any friend of Sage's is automatically a friend of mine." She enthusiastically shook Golem's hand.

Sage had Ro park in the Jeep slot and gave her one of the door openers. The two men carried Ro's luggage up to the unit.

The first item of business was to accede to Ro's demand to see the painting. While she was giving it her first minute inspection,

Sage poured the coffee and sat back to await Ro's approval, which he knew would be forthcoming. When it came to his work, Ro was not the unbiased observer she was on everything else.

The second item on the agenda was to right a Sage oversight. While he was on a commission, his only internet requirement was to occasionally check his email, which he did at wifi spots or at the library. Snapper did not have a computer, but the condo did have cable TV. Sage called the cable company to get a rush hookup to Roadrunner for Ro to conduct her research.

After coffee, Golem withdrew. However, Ro extracted a promise from him to return at margarita time. "I came all the way across the country for one of Sage's margaritas. That's a cause for celebration."

Sage and Ro spent the rest of the afternoon going over the homicide cases and Burke's problem. Ro was particularly interested in why Sage thought Snapper was not the murderer.

After a prolonged explanation, Ro summarized by saying, "In the end, it's a gut feeling. There's not a shred of evidence to support your position."

Sage sat for a long time before he replied. "You're right....but Snapper didn't do it."

"This discovery of the fresh body strengthens Burke's case....at least until Snapper reappears and provides evidence he didn't do it."

"Yeah, I wish he would check in. It's been weeks since he called Tinna."

"Do you think something has happened to him?"

"No, not really, but Golem and I had a bad moment when we found that stinky body."

Golem made it back for margaritas. This time he was in his working paint. Ro squealed with delight when she saw those blackened eyes. "Now here's man after my own heart. My hair keeps people from focusing on my size. With those eyes, no one will ever notice those knobby knees."

Golem looked down at his knees.

"Or anything else," said Ro with a laugh. "Now, where is my margarita? Golem have you ever had one of Sage's margaritas?"

"I'm pretty much a beer drinker."

"I realize that margaritas are an acquired taste but you shouldn't pass up the opportunity for a unique experience."

After considerable hesitation, Golem acceded to Ro's entreaties. "That's made out of tequila, right?"

"Ummm," intoned Ro.

"I don't think I've ever tasted that."

"If you don't like it," said Sage, "you can go back to beer. Then you can do like I do with persimmons and a number of other things. I don't particularly like persimmons, but I buy one each year so I can remind myself of why I don't like them. On occasions, I've developed a fondness for things on my list which is what happened to persimmons ."

Golem was indecisive concerning margaritas with the exception of "Boy, these are potent. Don't give me another one unless you want me to curl up in the corner."

After one margarita each, Sage offered to buy dinner at Jake's.

Sage pointed out that Dreadnought only had a front seat with two seatbelts.

Golem said, "My van only has two bucket seats." Both men smiled at Ro who was sporting a new, red muscle car.

"Fine," said Ro, "but I wasn't thinking about having a couple of soda straws as passengers. You'll just have scrunch up."

Dinner was well along before Jake put in an appearance. Sage and Golem immediately received the double pistol salute. The bench was in place by the time Jake had greeted other familiar faces. Jake acknowledged Ro's presence before transferring his bulk to the bench.

Sage made the introductions. "May I present Maria Angelic Guadalupe Rojas, which has been reduced to 'Ro.' Ro is an investigative freelancer looking into Snapper's case. Ro, this is Jake, our host and one of Snapper's longest standing friends. If you have any questions about Snapper, Jake would be the most likely to know the answer."

Ro's extended hand disappeared between Jake's thumb and forefinger. Jake dealt with that little hand as if it were fragile china. "This is indeed a pleasure little lady. I'm glad to see Sage has brought in a big gun to deal with our problem."

Both Ro and Sage raised questioning eyebrows.

"Golem told me about your website. That was a handsome piece of work."

Golem managed an off-center smile.

Jake continued, "The one question I can't answer and wish I could is, where is Snapper? Has anyone heard anything?"

All Jake got were negative shakes of the heads.

"I wish he'd get back here to defend himself. Burke is tossing out all sorts of innuendos, which are not being refuted. Eventually, those comments will become established knowledge and then become facts. That last body gave Burke new fodder for the rumor mill. I hear your cartoons are keeping him in a perpetual state of agitation and when he gets to hoppin' about, he blabs."

"Has he been to the Cowhunter Saloon?" said Sage.

"I don't think so but everyone seems to take great glee in describing each of those cartoons in excruciating detail, according to my sources."

"Humm," snorted Ro around a chunk of steak. Everyone had to wait until she masticated the meat enough to swallow. "You're back up to your old tricks, huh?" She grinned at Sage.

"Always trying to improve my skills," said Sage.

Golem and Jake looked blank.

Ro chuckled. "That's a story for another time, but you should see what his cartoons did to a US Senator."

Jake checked the surrounding area for eavesdroppers before saying, "One thing that concerns me is that Snapper had the bank deliver a big chunk of money for me to hold for him. I figured he'd need it by this time. Be sure to let me know if he wants it. I can get it to him." Jake stood up. It was time to greet other patrons.

When Sage motioned for the bill, there was none. He continued Snapper's routine of leaving an abundant tip.

At the condo Golem retrieved his van and headed home. Sage settled down to turn out some more cartoons. Ro disappeared into her room to get on the internet. At midnight Sage could hear the clicks of the keyboard, so he left the kitchen light on in case Ro wanted something. Sage headed for bed.

It was light out, but as far as Sage was concerned the day still had a ways to go before it needed his attention. That was his frame of mind when the phone rang. However, he couldn't not answer it. It was Hack.

"Turn on channel nine. I'll be back with you later." He didn't even wait for an answer before hanging up.

Sage turned on the small bedroom set to the weather report and then traffic. The "Breaking News" notice showed briefly before the morning anchor reported that an unknown shooter had tried to assassinate State Attorney, David Burke, last night as he sat on the balcony of his Orlando condo. As was his habit, Burke spent a few minutes relaxing on his patio-balcony before retiring. A shot by a high-powered firearm came from the ground level up to his second floor unity. The slug hit a vertical picket of the safety railing. The type or caliber of the gun is unknown because no casing was left and the projectile ricocheted off into space. Burke was shaken but unhurt. No one has reported seeing the assailant. The police are asking for the public's assistance. "Please call Crime Line if you saw anything suspicious around 11:30." The newscaster went on to give an address and description of the scene. As soon as the anchor passed onto another topic, Sage routed Ro out for the next cycle.

The coffee was ready before the report came up again. Sage and Ro sat in the living room to watch the big TV.

"Burke has already characterized Snapper," said Sage, "as a vicious throwback to a bygone lawless age. He's been digging into Snapper's colorful past and there are any number of episodes that may be completely unacceptable today. Burke will probably make a lot of hay out of this."

"So, you think that Snapper didn't do this. Who else would?" said Ro.

"First, we don't know if it's at all related to our case. Then this isn't Snapper's style of doing things. I think the shooter is the real killer."

"Your friend is a lot better suspect than anyone else. If the current theory is correct and Snapper is lurking somewhere on his ranch, it wouldn't be much of a trick to get to Orlando."

"I doubt if he is on the ranch. Although he can live off the land, why put up with the heat and the mosquitoes when you can buy anything you want?"

"Apparently you're the only one taking that viewpoint," said Ro. "Why do you think so?"

"Since I've been around, he's accepted his new addiction to air conditioning, microwaves and TV. He'd never had those before."

"Where would he go?"

"I have no idea, but I'd bet he has contacts all over the state and probably the country. He's done a lot of work with the Caribbean countries. He could be anywhere."

As additional information became available, it was reported that the crime scene investigators were working on the premise that it was an attempted homicide. After figuring the angles, they determined it would have been a fatal shot except for the metal bar, which would have not been visible to the shooter. It was reported that the States Attorney Burke would hold a press conference at 1:00 pm that afternoon.

While Ro was cooking huevos rancheros for breakfast, Hack called again. This time it was to Sage's cell phone. "Go outside and take a walk."

Sage stepped out on the walkway. Hack continued, "I don't think even Burke would risk tapping an attorney's phone, but he might do it on Snapper's or put a bug in the condo. Have you heard from our friend? This is important."

"Not a peep. Jake asked the same question. He's holding money for Snapper, which hasn't been picked up. I think Jake is afraid something has happened to Snapper."

"Well, if he checks in, impress on him the importance of getting in touch with me."

When Sage broke the connection, he was standing at the east end of the walkway overlooking the parking lot and pool. There was a little tug on his right shirtsleeve. He flinched in surprise. It was Mona.

"Mona, good morning."

"They're back."

"Who are?"

"Those official cars are back in the parking lot but the guys are not in the same unit. It's been sold. There's another vacancy one floor down and one unit to the left."

"Why, thank you, Mona. You're a doll."

Mona ducked her head, blushed furiously and skittered back to her condo.

Sage returned to his unit. With Snapper's binoculars he located the spies right where Mona had indicated. Ro, standing back in the shadows, watched the watchers. "This could be fun," she said.

Both went back to their own projects. They took a short break for lunch. At margarita time Golem showed up. When Sage came out of his room to meet Golem, the living room was gloomy. All the hurricane shutters had been lowered but not clamped shut. That let in a modicum of light.

Ro came out of her room with a broad smile, demanding a margarita. Golem opted for a beer. Sage returned to his martini.

The petite redhead was harboring a plan, which she wouldn't divulge until drinks were served. Then she led the way out to the gloomy deck. Sage noted a large stack of boxes at the far end, that weren't a normal part of the décor. Ro remained mute on the subject. The conversation reverted back to the Snapper situation, which continued through a refill and until the sun had set.

Ro upended her glass and licked off the remaining salt. "I'll be back in a moment."

Both guys looked at one another and shrugged.

Shortly, Ro reappeared, barefooted and wearing a short robe. "Come on, guys, it's sauna-time." At the end of the deck were two doors. Sage knew that one was a storage area and tool shed because Snapper had retrieved a hammer from there. He figured that the other one was also storage.

Ro opened the door to a blast of hot air. She gave the hot rocks a squirt of water causing steam to billow out the door. "Shed those clothes and enjoy." She slipped out of her robe and stood in the nude, waiting.

Sage laughed and started to strip. Golem just watched, wide-eyed.

"Come on, Golem, get with it," chided Ro. "If you ever visit the Hacienda, you'll have to contend with the unisex bathroom. You might as well start your training now."

In slow motion, Golem began to unbutton his shirt. He was still working on the shirt when Sage stepped out of his trousers. As Golem was removing his shirt, Ro moved forward to unbutton and unzip his walking shorts. Hooking her thumbs in at the waist, she peeled the rest of his clothes down to his sandals.

Ro led the way into the sauna. She tossed each of the guys a towel from a stack she'd stashed beside the door. Golem immediately started to wrap the towel around his nakedness. Ro snatched the towel away. "To sit on, unless you have an asbestos butt."

Golem laid the towel on the bench and sat down, but he still was able to drag a corner of it up over his crotch, while all three watched the terry cloth begin to tent.

"Golem."

"What?"

"Your mascara is running."

Figuring the emergency was lower on his body, Golem had to suddenly reevaluate his area of concern.

Ro was watching black rivulets roll down his cheeks. A big grimy drop had formed on his chin. When it fell, it left a dark trail down his flat abdomen, which disappeared under the tent. Golem snatched up the towel to control the new assault on his dignity, abandoning the former crisis. After mopping up the liquefied pigment, Golem tossed the dirty towel on the bench and plopped down on it to the chuckles of the two others.

When the trio had sweated sufficiently, Sage said, "There are three showers in this place. The master bedroom has a his and hers in the grand bath. Ro and I will take those two. Golem, you can use my shower. Take care....there may be three showers, but only one hot water tank."

When Sage finished his shower, he returned to the patio, which was now brightly lighted by the house lights flooding through the sliders. Ro was there with a towel wrapped around her hair and another around her body.

"What's up?" asked Sage.

"Thought it might be fun to put on a little show for our peeping toms. With those shutters set in the light mode, they can't see in but they can see shadows pass over those little holes. If we move around a bit, they should have fun trying to count shadows, and if we close all other window shades, it might give them something to think about."

"Yeah," said Sage. "They might think Snapper's hiding in here and come calling."

"That all right. He's not here. That's just more egg on their face. That's the name of the game right now, isn't it?"

"Well, true," said Sage. "That's the only game we have until some new information comes along."

The three spent a few minutes casting shadows in random patterns against the deck shutters.

Finally Ro said, "You've been bragging about the Surf Restaurant. Are you going to take me there tonight for dinner?"

"Not like that. You've got half an hour to get yourself together."

Ro countered with, "Forty minutes. You may be bigger than me but I've got more hair, even if you count your legs."

The time estimate had been about right. Ro emerged from her room in a stunning, provocative black party dress designed to be a conversation stopper in even the worldliest environments. In Cocoa Beach, Ro would be stunning without jewelry or accessories. Sage and Golem assessed each other's attire. "Boy, are we the ugly ducklings," said Sage.

"I'm introducing myself to the local crowds," said Ro. "You guys are already known quantities. Let go, I'm hungry."

While the three-some was waiting for the elevator, Sage noticed a guy on the lower patio, who was ostensibly smoking a cigarette. If the smoker had looked around to see who was calling the elevator, Sage wouldn't have taken any particular notice, but a quick surreptitious glance aroused Sage's interest, especially under the circumstances.

"Wait for me," said Sage in a loud enough voice to carry to the patio. "I forgot my wallet."

Sage hustled back to the unit. The blinds were still drawn in the kitchen. Sage knew that the phone numbers of the other condo residents were on a card in the drawer below the phone. He looked up and then dialed a number, using his cell phone.

"Hi Mona. This is Sage. My friends and I are going out for dinner. Could you kind of keep an eye on this place to see if any one messes around? If so, don't do anything except note the time and what happened on this date on your calendar. Got to go now, thanks."

As he was relocking the door, he slipped a tiny scrap of paper into the hinge side of the door. Moments later he slipped into the elevator, which Golem was holding.

Ro's introduction to Cocoa Beach was a raving success. When the teeny redhead made an entrance through the bar entrance escorted by two very tall young males, the patrons took notice. A hostess quickly cleared the only empty table. It was a round table in the corner. Ro slid into the middle so she could be flanked by her pair of escorts.

They ordered drinks. Golem placed a reservation for a table in the dining room. Periodically, most of the young men who had no girlfriends or wives in tow came by to say hello to Golem so they could be introduced to the current celebrity. Ro was having a wonderful time.

Word had reached the dining room, so as they were shown their table, everyone charted their progress across the room. Ro's introduction to the local scene probably stimulated a lot of conversations.

When the group returned to the condo, Golem picked up his van and headed home. Sage checked the door for his paper. It was missing. Someone had opened the door during their absence. Sage checked out all the rooms before taking a hike with his cell phone.

Mona hissed at him as he went by her unit. She remained inside her screen door in the shadows. Sage leaned against the rail as if making a phone call. "Hi, Mona."

In a low voice his neighbor said. "Thirty-three minutes after you left, two men opened the door with a key. They were inside eleven minutes. I didn't see them leave the property so they may still be around somewhere." Mona giggled before continuing. "I've got it all written down on my calendar. I even wrote down as good a description as I can get."

"Thanks, Mona, you're a doll." More giggling as the door closed.

"Hack, this is Sage." The painter related the chain of events concerning the surveillance and the unforced entry. "Also, they were in here an awful long time just to see if Snapper was hiding under the bed."

"If you don't already have a journal, start one. Write down times and events that may have some relationship to this case. If this thing ever goes to trial, I'd like to be able to ask questions about unlawful entries. Write it all down so you can refresh your memory at a later date. Have you heard anything from Snapper?"

"No, nothing."

"Clay told me that there is no longer an active search but there are watchers to report on anyone who moves. Clay's ranch hands are getting rather jumpy. They'd like to shoot a few of those bastards who are continually popping up from behind every other bush."

"It sounds as if Burke is getting rather spastic. I understand he's running out of money. All of this surveillance stuff should be ruining his budget."

"Right," said Hack, with a nasty chuckle. "Surveillance is not a normal budgetary item for a states attorney."

The next morning, Sage passed the time making a drawing of the now well-established caricature of Burke with a bandit's mask, picking a lock on Snapper's condo. Ro was deep in her research on the internet.

When the phone rang, Sage checked the Caller ID. He didn't recognize the source, so he let the answering machine pick up the call. It turned out to be Golem asking Sage to answer if he was in.

"Hi, what's up?"

"Say, Arty's in town....hiding from Burke. We're going to the Beach Shanty for a beer. Bring Ro along and meet us."

Sage transmitted the invitation to Ro, who looked tempted but said, "I'm right in the middle of something. I'll pass. I don't want to lose the train of thought. Another time."

His friends were already at their regular back table. Sage picked up a Coors as he passed the bar.

"Ro is in the middle of something. She'll see you another day." To Arty, Sage said, "You're making weekday visits a regular habit."

"I'm going to blame it all on you."

"Me?"

"Every morning Burke calls someone to get a report on the latest cube cartoon. From that time on, he's in a foul mood. He figures misery needs a bedfellow and I don't want to go to bed with that negative a person. So, I'm hiding."

"Was it you guys or law enforcement who let themselves into Snapper's last night?"

Arty took a swig of beer and looked uncomfortable. "You know I can't answer that question."

Sage shrugged and changed the question. "Burke made it very clear in his statement the other day that he was certain the new body was the work of the same individual. How can he be so sure?"

"There are plenty of factors available to make that determination. The binding cord this time was different than all the former ones but the way it was wrapped and the knots used to tie the whole thing together are identical."

Arty's laptop was lying on the chair next to him. He activated the computer and selected a file before swinging it around for Sage to see. The screen had a shot of the last body package lying on the morgue table. Sage recognized the object, but he had not examined it closely. Now, without the horrid odor he could look more closely. Arty pointed out where cords had been put around the blanket wrapped body. He counted the number of wraps. There was a close-up of the knots used and how the loose ends were tied off to keep them from flopping around.

Arty took the computer back to locate another file. When the screen was turned back to Sage and Golem, Sage sucked air across his teeth loudly enough for Arty and Golem to look at him. Sage grimaced. "I'm hoping I can wait to get home to my dentist. When I drink something cold, a tooth gets sensitive. Sorry for the interruption. What do we have here?"

"This is the first body. Look at the ties on this one. They're almost identical to all the rest, including the latest. Here are close-ups of the knots....the same....the cords on the first twenty appear to be hay bale ties of hemp. The new one is nylon cord.

As Arty started to shut down the machine, Sage said, "Go back to the first bundle. Does the killer show any color preference? The last bundle that Golem and I found was blue. What color was this one?

Arty checked the file. "This one was natural, uncolored wool. With all those years in the ground there was a lot of oxidation has taking place. There has to be a chemical analysis to be sure."

"There's a pattern on the wool blanket. That looks similar to a stylized wave. What color was that?"

Arty read through the written material. "The wave thing was

yellow with red dots."

Golem was watching Sage intently. Sage gave him a small, almost imperceptible shake of the head as Arty shut down his computer.

Sage finished his beer but declined a second. "It won't be long before Ro surfaces, yelling for a margarita. For dinner, we may try that seafood place on the causeway down from A-1-A. Someone suggested it. Join us if you're able."

As Sage passed out the door, he paused to look at the beach before sauntering up the ramp to the street. As soon as he was out of sight of the Beach Shanty, he quickened his pace back to Dreadnought.

"Ro," yelled Sage as he entered the condo.

The redhead, dressed only in shorts and a halter top stuck her head out of the bedroom. "What's up?"

"We've got a problem. I just saw a photo of the first body. It was wrapped in that blanket....or one just like it." Sage was pointing at the Indian blanket thrown over the homemade chair in Sage's painting. "That blanket was in Snapper's house years before the first murder."

"Are you sure it's the same blanket?"

"It's supposed to be an Indian blanket and I don't imagine that there was any mass manufacturing in those days."

"What are you going to do?"

"First, I'm going to paint out that design. A lot of people have seen the painting but probably only a few really looked at it since I added the design. If someone had made the connection between the murder blanket and the painting, we'd have heard of it by now. Oh, Golem knows. He recognized it as soon I inquired into the colors, but he didn't say anything at the time. I hope he sees me first before he mentions it to Arty."

"This makes your theory a little more untenable doesn't it?"

"On the face of it, yes. I can't really tell until I learn more about that blanket."

Ro and Sage were having after-dinner coffee at the seafood place when Golem showed up.

"Couldn't get away any earlier. Arty wanted to eat at the Cuban eatery south of town. He's on his way back home."

When Golem finished his speech, he continued to sit straight and look expectant.

"You saw what I saw today?" said Sage.

"Yeah. You mean the blanket?"

"Right. I've eliminated it from the painting. Most of the troops that trudge through in early stages of the investigation were there before I put the pattern in. Burke and several deputy SAs have seen it in various forms as well as some police officers but no one has apparently made the connection."

"That doesn't look good for Snapper," said Golem.

"No, not good, but let's get an explanation before we jump on Burke's bandwagon. Boy, I wish Snapper would check in."

Before heading for bed, Sage was checking the late TV news so see if anything had happened pertaining to Snapper's case. The phone rang. The Caller ID showed it was Tinna. She was so excited she could hardly get through the pleasantries before blurting, "I just got a call...."

Sage broke in, "Great. I'll let you tell me on my nickel. I'll call you right back."

Sage stepped out on the walkway and punched up Tinna's number. She picked up immediately.

"What did he have to say?"

"He kept it very brief. He said to have you tell Hack that he's been out of the country continuously since right after the run-in with Burke at the bank and that he can prove it. He said as soon as Burke squashes that warrant he'll come home. That's all he said. He didn't tell me where he was. He sounded good."

"What did the Caller ID indicate?

"Unknown caller."

"I'm glad he's all right," said Sage. "It's too late to call Hack. He can't do anything until tomorrow anyway."

For the second time that day Sage yelled for Ro as he went back into the condo. She was actually standing a few feet from his right shoulder waiting for tea water to heat.

"What's up?"

Sage jumped, not expecting her to be so close. He motioned her out onto the patio. "Tinna just received a call from Snapper." He repeated what Tinna had reported.

"If Snapper can prove he was out of the country the whole time," said Ro, "That would help clear him of personally committing the last two crimes. However, I'll bet Burke will take the position that Snapper could have hired it done. His being out of the country doesn't clear him of the first twenty murders."

"You're right. The key to this whole thing may be that blanket. Of course, there may be two similar blankets, and Snapper's daughter-in-law or someone else still has it in a trunk. Nuts, I've got to talk to Snapper. Tomorrow I'll call Tinna and have her try to impress Snapper that I need to talk to him.

Chapter 12

Hack was an early riser, so Sage rolled out sooner than normal. He wanted to get the show rolling.

After Sage told Hack of the call, the attorney was silent for an extended time but let Sage know the line was still open by swiping the phone across his stubble.

"Burke is never going to voluntarily squelch—not squash—that warrant. Every time he hears the name Snapper, or your name, for that matter, he gets a facial tick. He has too much of his very essence tied up in this case to back away now. He's loaded his entire legal future onto one horse. I'll see what I can do, but the prospects are not good. I'll let you know."

Sage didn't tell Hack about the blanket. He figured he'd let the attorney focus all of his attention on the chore at hand. Sage knew that Hack strongly believed that his old friend hadn't committed those atrocities. There was no sense in diluting his persuasive efforts with disquieting information.

It turned out to be a thoroughly unsettled morning as Ro and Sage awaited the verdict from Hack. It wasn't until 4:00 in the afternoon that the call came in.

"Burke won't budge. He is demanding that Snapper turn himself in first and then the SA will look at any evidence Snapper wants to present. I even told him he could refile the charges anytime he has enough evidence to win. I think he feels that to vacate his original assumptions would be admitting failure. This he isn't going to do."

"I'll pass your word along. We'll have to see what Snapper wants to do."

At martini time, Golem showed up. They took their assorted drinks to the patio, where Ro and Sage filled in the story for the woodcarver. A gloom spread over the bunch.

"I'm going to have to bundle up my goodies and head for home soon," said Sage. "I can't afford to delay much longer. I need to get back to work."

"My background research is almost complete," said Ro. "I need to get into the police files and I can't while there is a pending case. As it stands now, there isn't enough of interest to make this a marketable story."

Suddenly, Sage jumped up. "Idiot!" he said with feeling. "I need to shoot new photos of that room. All of mine show that blanket design. Ro, please close the storm shutters. If there are any watchers, we'll let them think we're taking another sauna. Golem, help me move the table and chairs out of the way."

For an hour, Sage reshot all his photos of the finished project. Then he bundled the chip of the original photos, along with any prints he'd made that showed the chair and blanket. These he put in a mailer to Tinna. After the room was returned to its normal state, Sage took a walk to call Tinna.

"There's a large envelope coming your way. Please put it in a hole. I've got bad news for our friend." Sage gave her the information from Hack. "Also tell him I need to talk to him most urgently. I'll be leaving here probably by the weekend. I can't stay around here forever."

"Good. Get back here soon. I want one of your martinis."

When Sage went back inside, Ro was on the house phone saying, "This is Ro, the Red Flea. You know who I am?.....good. It's time we small people met face to face. At 2:00 tomorrow afternoon, you go into the Cowhunter Saloon and select a table as private as you can get. Order me a mug of dark. I'll be there by the time the coffee is drinking temperature....Postpone that hearing. This is more important. Don't be late." Ro hung up.

Golem had a very crooked smile.

"Was that who I think it was?"

"You mean Burke? Yes. This whole affair is getting nowhere. I figure it was about time I straightened him out. I will need an escort tomorrow afternoon. Are you two men available?"

"I wouldn't miss this for all the palm logs in Florida," said Golem.

"Whatever the lady wishes." said Sage.

"Be sure to wear your cowboy....western boots. Golem, do you have any tall boots?"

"No."

"Okay, wear your heeled sandals and your war paint. I want a couple of tallllllllll escorts."

"Oh boy, we're in for an entertaining day."

At 1:30 the following afternoon, the red Mustang was sitting in the parking lot across the road. Ro was dressed in tight pants and a matching tank top. They, matched her hair. A black tie held her waist-long hair in a ponytail. She was wearing flats so she wouldn't be taller than her invited guest. A narrow black belt around her petite waist completed her ensemble

An official car pulled into the parking lot with ten minutes to spare. Burke and two other men climbed out of the car. Burke had been driving because he needed a built-up seat that no one else could use. The trio entered the coffee house.

"We'll wait here until he can get seated. I want to enter with a hand on each of your arms. As I understand it, the counter is on the left and the boot-black stand is on the right. When we get inside, I'll leave you guys. Get coffee and take seats on the stand. From there on out we'll play it by ear."

Sage led the way through the door followed by Ro and Golem.

Inside Ro took the two arms and steered the trio about half way down the bar. Burke was at a rear corner table but with a view of the door.

Ro said, "Shoo," and advanced on her own to meet Burke, who had popped to his feet. There were a number of expressions trying to play across his face. The tick won out as he glanced back at Ro's companions.

The redhead marched around the table so she could stand almost nose-to-nose with the SA. Burke was a little bit taller. Ro stuck out her hand and said, "Mister Burke, I'm glad you could make it."

Miss Rojas," said the attorney.

There were two coffee mugs on the table across from one another. Instead of going to the other side of the table, she moved her cup to the chair next to Burke's.

Suddenly, Burke remembered his manners as Ro stood next to the chair waiting to be seated. Though belatedly, Burke performed the procedure efficiently.

Ro slowly surveyed the room. The two deputies were seated at a nearby table trying to look detached from the Burke/Ro proceedings.

"You might want to send your men either out or to a more discrete distance. We're going to have a private talk that I'm sure you won't want heard by anyone. If you're wired, I think you might want to get rid of it." Ro smiled sweetly.

Burke looked toward his men and jerked his head calling one over. Burke removed a pocket handkerchief and handed it to the deputy. "Go sit with Grayling."

Turning to Ro, the attorney said, "I'm here and you have your stage set the way you want it. Now is it going to be a comedy or tragedy?"

"Right now it's a poor comedy, working its way toward a tragedy and you're the main character."

Burke started to bristle.

"Stop it," hissed Ro. "You and I have the same battle to fight every day. I'm winning and you're losing. The reason for that is you are trying to prove you're just as much a man as anyone who wears a jockstrap, or better if you can manage it. You use people to make yourself tall."

Burke jumped up sending his chair careening against the wall. "You don't know anything about me."

"You'd be surprised what I know about you," said Ro in her same low, steady voice. "For instance you wear navy blue, low-rise briefs and you're circumcised. Now sit down."

Burke looked around. Everyone was watching the proceeding, but fortunately they couldn't hear.

Ro took a sip of her hot coffee but she didn't put the mug down. "See, you're play acting again. Sit down or I'll flip the coffee into your crotch and then you can try to explain to everyone how you didn't actually pee your pants."

Burke retrieved his chair and sat down rubbing his left leg as if he'd had a spasm.

"Quit it. You're trying to wiggle your way out of a temper tantrum by acting as if it was a muscular problem brought about by too arduous a physical training regime. Now let's get down to business.

"The difference between the two of us is that you're continually fighting your size. On the other hand, I've accepted mine and have turned it to my advantage. Of course I have the advantage that I am a cute woman. But, you're a good-looking man. We both are put together on the same pattern as anyone else, except smaller.

"I've gone into a field, investigative reporting, where size makes no difference. My bylines don't include my height. I've been able to use my size to great advantage. I go places and do things that would be barred to normal sized women. I don't constitute a physical threat to anyone. If I'm a threat, it's because of my mind.

"On the other hand, you have chosen a profession where size counts. You are in a public office where everyone is critically watched. You don't have to do a thing and you already have one strike against you.... 'he's too tiny to be of any account'.

"I know you're bright...."

"And how do you know that?" sneered Burke.

"I have your high school and college transcripts and one of your grade school report cards where Miss Mitchell writes that you fight too much."

"How did you get that?" demanded the attorney.

"I've been trying to tell you that I'm good at what I do. But, let's get back to the main subject of this affair....you. Not only have you entered a profession where you have to daily compete, but your future is dependent on big men—the politicians—for your continued existence."

"I don't serve anyone except the people in my jurisdiction."

"Don't give me a campaign speech," said Ro. "If you want to get reelected you have to be in favor with the Democrats to get their money, backing and slave labor. Even if you win, you lose. I will probably pay more income tax this year than you make."

"Money isn't everything."

"But it's nice." said Ro with a beatific smile. "If you want to continue in law, you'd be far better off using the time before the campaign quietly looking around in an area far away from here for a position in a law firm that wants what's between your ears instead of a big chest measurement–a firm that handles big, challenging cases. Become a top line expert in a lucrative field. Get paid for what you know, not how loudly you can pound your chest."

Burke's slow burn had subsided somewhat and he appeared to be listening, although he had to be quieted periodically by Ro raising a finger as he drew in a deep breath to speak.

"Finally, there is one other thing you'd better know. See that tall fellow sitting on the end of the shoe shine thing? Don't screw around with him. I've seen what his creative mind did to a Senator, Governor and State Chief Justice when he turned it loose on them. I've also heard stories about a sheriff that tried to screw around with him. All he's doing now is drawing a few cartoons to put in a cube in one coffee house. Oh, he got the idea for the cube from your desk. If he decides to expand his viewership, by tomorrow he could go national. You've seen his website.

"At the moment his only stake in this is that he thinks that you are not giving his boss and now friend a fair shake on this murder business. Snapper is not going to let you throw him in jail. So this will not be resolved before the election, and by that time Sage could make the name Burke a pejorative. Sage, the guy up in front, is not trying to evade justice. He just wants his friend to be judged fairly."

Ro was so busy plowing through her talking points, she misinterpreted the subtle changes in the attitude of her audience. Suddenly, she realized Burke wasn't intently listening to her remarks, but he was intently watching her moves and scrutinizing her attributes.

"Stop it," commanded Ro in her most authoritative voice. She banged her mug loudly on the table for emphasis. Burke jumped. "Do you think I'd hook up with a loser? Right now you look like a hopeless case, to me. You're not going to capture Snapper. Sage is going to make you a ridiculous looking figure and you'll lose the next election. You're not my type. Besides, I have a nice, young Chicano who would brace the gates of Hades for me if he even suspected that would please me. When my ego needs fortification or my libido needs a massage, I stop by Albuquerque for a very satisfactory treatment. Afterward, we are both free to continue our own respective pursuits.

"You'd better get your act together or you'll continue to have your mother laundering your dirty shorts and sitting alone at night on the balcony of an economy condo."

Before Burke had a chance to respond Ro was on her feet and headed for her escorts. She smiled benignly at the deputy SAs before she took the arms of Sage and Golem.

Chapter 13

—m—

Sage was sitting on the foot of the monstrous bed in the master bedroom as Ro finished her packing. Shortly, she was going to head for Orlando airport to return to San Francisco.

"This has been fun but so far there is no story. I'll just hold onto everything until there is a resolution. Even with a trial and conviction there really isn't anything for an ebook. It might warrant consideration in a true crime mag or an anthology, if anyone is putting them out any more."

"Sorry I wasted your time," said Sage.

"Oh, there was no wasted time. This was just a Florida vacation with a good friend. I hope that stone-skulled Burke heard some of what I said. I think he's probably a good person. If he could stop fighting the world, he might let a little goodness soak through. There still may be a story here yet."

The phone rang. Sage was inclined to let the answering machine pick up the call. He didn't want to deal with anything just then. He was also leaving all sorts of unfinished business. A depressive gloom seemed to ooze out of all the condo nooks and crannies.

"Sage, give me a call," came out of the answering machine. Sage jumped for the phone. "Hack, I'm here."

"Good. I was afraid you'd already left. I don't know what you did to Burke, but he called this morning to say he would withdraw the warrant on Snapper and listen to what he had to say. Burke said he would not take action on his own but he'd continue his investigation. When the inquiry is complete he'll take his findings to the grand jury if he feels such an action is warranted.

"I asked him to reduce his plan of action to writing and send it to me. He balked at first but eventually agreed. There is one stipulation....you have to cease and desist from drawing those cartoons. The letter should be in my hand by the end of the day. So get the word out and keep me posted." Hack hung up.

As Sage was relaying the message to Ro, she began to unpack. "Don't want to abandon the battlefield before the battle."

Sage called Tinna.

Later that night, Tinna called to report Snapper had called in and he'd gotten the message. "He said he'd be coming in but he wouldn't say how or when."

For two days Sage and Ro haunted the condo, waiting. Golem dropped in at margarita time. They were seated on the patio when Snapper let himself in the front door and waved for the trio to stay put. "I'll pick up a bourbon and ranch water and join you. After handshakes, Sage introduced Ro, who instantly won another admirer.

Of course, the first order of business was for Snapper to tell where he'd been.

"After that dust-up at the bank with Burke, I decided I'd better not make myself too available. Before leaving the bank, I ordered some financial arrangements. Then I went to the grocery store where I bought a ton of camp grub. I spent a little time at the ranch laying down some fake trails.

"Then I went to a friend's house on Merritt Island. He and his wife spend the summer up north. I have a blanket permission to use the house any time I want to. The house, with all its comforts, was a lot better than camping on the ranch, but the thought of being cooped up in there for weeks or maybe months didn't appeal to me.

"To pass time, I was reading through a stack of travel brochures. One struck my fancy. I poked around until I found Arn's stuff that he leaves here when he goes north. In his bedside drawer were the papers for the older Lexus in the garage, Florida driver's license and a stack of Florida credit cards.

"That night I was heading south to Miami. I stuck the Lexus on a ferry boat and we were off for Belize. I became Arn Ruck. I found a parking lot in Belize City and boarded a gambling ship. I've been on that ship until I talked with Tinna the other night. I have all the documentation to prove it and nice little chunk of winnings to boot."

Sage got up to make another round of drinks while Ro and Golem filled Snapper in on all the developments since his departure.

"From the ship, I could keep track of what the Sentinel had to say about the murders. It was a great life. Sleep when you want, eat at any time and gamble all the time. I pretty much kept to the poker tables. Never take too much off the table and tip well, and one is always welcome. When we'd get back in port, I'd pay the fee on my cabin and sleep until the dining room and tables opened again.

"Okay, that's my story. How'd Hack get Burke to kill that warrant?"

"It was probably Ro who tipped the scale," said Sage. "She had a little talk with him and he's doing back flips to please her."

"What did you have promise him to make him so agreeable?" asked Snapper.

Ro laughed. "I didn't promise anything. I cajoled and threatened. He thinks I know his life's history after I told him I knew he wore navy blue low-rise briefs and he was circumcised."

Snapper nearly choked on his drink. "How'd you know that?

"I drove by his mother's house. She does his laundry and she doesn't wear those tiny blue shorts. The other was an educated guess. Burke is a shortening of Burkestein. The name was changed a couple of generations back when being a Jew was tough. His mother goes to synagogue so I figured his parents followed tradition."

"There had to be more to it than that," pressed Snapper.

"Oh, as one small person to another, I read him the riot act on his actions and I predicted his immanent professional demise if he held his course. Some of what I said must have stuck."

"Okay," said Sage, "back to the problem at hand. Golem, please turn on the dining room lights and move that easy chair behind the davenport and center it on the dining room."

"Good," injected Snapper. "I want to see the finished painting."

"The group moved into the shadowy living room. Golem turned on the lights.

"Snapper, please sit down in the chair and look at the painting."

Snapper complied. As he scanned the painting from the prime vantage point of a trompe-l'oeil painting, he said, "Ooh, great, wonderful. It looks like the real thing. It certainly brings back a flood of memories."

The examination continued until Snapper said, "What happened to the red dots?"

"Tell me about that blanket."

"There's nothing to tell. As I recall it belonged to one of the ranch hands. He didn't want to leave it in the bunkhouse. Someone would steal it to buy a drink or two. So he left it at the big house. He must have picked it up when he left. Why?"

"Do you remember when that was or anything about the owner?"

"Hell, that was when I was just a kid. That's a long time ago. I can't recall anything about the owner, if I ever knew who it was in the first place. It wasn't on the chair very long"

"Why was it on the chair?"

"There wasn't much storage in that house, so mom tossed it over that ugly chair."

"Did you ever see it after that?"

"No. What's this all about?"

"That blanket or one like it was used to cover the first body in your little graveyard. I was able to get a look at some of the sheriff's pictures and I recognized the pattern. So, to keep thing from getting worse, I painted out the design on the blanket."

"I don't recall anything about the blanket, other than it was there."

"Now we have another suspect for the murders," said Golem.

"If it shows up on the first body that dates back to 1948, it would have been in your house prior to that. Are there any records that would identify that ranch hand?"

"We don't have records that go that far back. Then the pay roll records would have only said Pete or Snake....so much. Everything was cash and pretty casual."

"What happens when a hand leaves the ranch?" said Ro.

"Oh, he goes to another ranch, if he hasn't already worn out his welcome in the territory. If he has, he drifts off."

"Without a name, he'd be hard to trace," said Golem.

"I'd be willing to bet we now have our killer." said Sage. "We've found another person here at the start of the killings. And the killer knows Snapper knows him. That was the motive behind the attempt on Snapper's life. When Snapper wasn't available, the killer killed again and tried to shoot Burke in an attempt to further implicate Snapper. Now all we have to do is find him."

Ro excused herself to move her things out of Snapper's room into Sage's. Snapper objected putting the two of them together.

"Don't worry," said Ro, "We've spent a lot of nights together on our last little adventure. Besides if he doesn't behave himself, I'll tell Tinna."

"Sometime I'm going to have to meet Tinna," said Snapper. "She's a lot of fun to talk to over the phone. I'm buying at Jake's. The food on the gambling ship was supposed to be some of the best in the world, but it all seemed prechewed with a sauce over it. I can hardly wait to snuggle up to one of Jake's T-bones."

Before the group departed for Jake's, some vehicle juggling was necessary. Ro moved her Mustang outside so Snapper could get his Jeep in the garage. "Sorry about dispossessing you, but I smuggled my winnings into the country and they're stashed in the Jeep."

Finally, everyone piled into the Caddy with Golem behind the wheel. When the quartet entered Jake's, the decibels dropped. It was difficult to tell whether it was Snapper's presence, or the tiny redhead being escorted by the tall rangy guy or the black-eyed, gaunt stick-figure. Whatever the impetus, Jake's staff fell to, in order to seat Snapper and his entourage. Sage noted that the head waiter was immediately on the phone. Sage would have bet the farm that the call was to alert Jake.

Sage smiled as the bench arrived with the drinks, and Jake wasn't far behind. "Ah, old friend, has Jake lost favor with you? You have been gone for so long."

"I was trying to see if I could go two months without one of your steaks, but I couldn't do it."

Everyone laughed and the story telling began. Jake stayed on throughout the meal. As the plates were being cleared and the coffee cups were being refilled, Jake motioned to the headwaiter, who brought a small satchel to the table.

"This is the package that was delivered by a bank messenger," said Jake as he handed it to Snapper.

"Thanks for hanging on to it for me. As it happened, I didn't need it." Snapper slid the satchel across the table to Sage. "Split this up between the three of you to help cover the costs of taking care of my interests while I was sitting around making more of this stuff."

Not knowing what was in the package, but suspecting that it was cash, Sage accepted the bag and said, "Three ways." He'd wait until he found out what he was dealing with before saying more.

As Jake was gathering himself to rise, he said, "Well, old friend, it's good to see you back."

"Just how old is your friendship," asked Sage.

"We go way back. The Circle K was my first job," said Jake.

"When was that?"

"That was just at the end of the war. I was too young and looked even younger so I couldn't even fib my way into the army. Snapper's dad gave me a job helpin' with the horses."

"Do you happen to remember a guy who worked on the Circle K about that same time who owned a fancy yellowish colored Indian blanket?"

"No, that doesn't scrape up any memories."

"He probably stayed around this area for several years."

"Most of the guys eventually moved on. Some got out of the business like Arn and me."

"How'd you get out of the business?" asked Ro.

"I used to help the cook, and sometimes he'd get so drunk he couldn't put out a meal, so I'd do the cookin'. Old man Keel got tired of that lush. He canned the cook and switched me into the kitchen.

"That's hard work. Day starts before down and lasts until well after dark. Those guys want to eat seven days a week. Later, I quit and went to cookin' in town."

"Did you ever run into any of ex Circle K hands?" said Sage.

"Sure. Lots of them."

"Ones that stayed around for a long time?"

"Yeah. There was Arn, who had the feed and seed. There was Pete who bought and sold horses until business dried up. He moved on. Wayne worked in the hardware store until he died in a car crash. I went to his funeral. That tall, skinny guy with the big mustache had a barber shop on the beach for years. There was another guy....can't remember his name....that went next door to Braxton's. He worked his way to foreman because he was so big and tough. Later he got into some sort of physical conditioning thing. Remember Hazy, the clown? He went into car sales after the war and then switched to insurance. He made a fortune. Most of the guys I knew on the ranch moved on down the road after Circle K. Over the years there have been hundreds who have drawn pay from the Circle K. You think one of them is the killer?"

Sage shrugged. "I know Snapper didn't do in those boys. Someone else with a connection to the ranch did."

Snapper had been silent through the whole conversation. "It

seems I remember a big, burly guy who used to ramrod the Braxton place. Braxton owned the ranch on the north side of the Circle K. That's the side of the lake with the graveyard. On our property lines was a large cattle-handling area for shipping. Braxton and my dad went together to put in the corrals and loading shoots instead of each putting one in their own. That big guy was really young for the job, but no one was tough enough to take it away from him."

"Remember his name?" asked Sage.

"No. Maybe it'll come later. Of course, the chances are I only knew a nickname."

On the ride home, Sage asked Snapper, "Are there any records that would have the big guy's name?"

"I wouldn't have any. All the records that far back would have been hand written in notebooks. Florida weather and bugs makes short work of paper. It wasn't until years later....after dad died.... that we ever took out withholding tax. Someone will just have to remember it."

When they returned to the condo Golem accompanied the group upstairs. He joined Sage and Ro in their room to open the package Snapper had given them.

All were astonished that there was $50,000 in small bills. "I knew Jake was holding some money for Snapper,' said Sage, "but I was thinking in the realm of $5,000, plus or minus....not this amount. This is too much."

They all trouped out of the bedroom to tell Snapper that his generosity was excessive, but before they could register their thoughts, Snapper intervened. "I don't want to hear your estimate of the value that I should place on your support and assistance for the last few weeks. Besides, while I was living the life of luxury, I more than replaced that amount. There is no way of tracing the money. I could have lost it gambling while out of the country, so you don't even have to declare it unless you are foolish enough to deposit it in a bank."

Snapper grinned and picked up his bourbon as he headed for his bedroom. "It will be good to sleep in my own bed again."

In the morning, Sage called Arty Misconi to arrange a meeting between him and Snapper. Sage was also going to be there. Sage didn't want to risk a direct interview with Burke. If the SA stepped out of line, Snapper might squash him. Besides, Hack would have to be present at such an event. This little get-together was to take place at the Beach Shanty at 10:00 the following morning.

Sage spent the rest of the day repainting the wave pattern and the cad red dots. Ro was repacking and making new arrangements to return to San Francisco. Then she decided she needed a sabbatical in Albuquerque. She cancelled the airline reservation and made arrangements to turn in her rental car in Cocoa Beach so she could ride back with Sage.

Just before martini time, Sage cleaned up his painting mess and was returning equipment to Dreadnought when Mona sneaked up on him again. With a pluck at his right sleeve she said, "You've got another watcher."

Sage's immediate reaction was, *That dirty bastard,* meaning Burke.

Before he could complete the framing of his indignant reaction, Mona continued, "This one isn't government."

"What do you mean?"

"The car isn't an official one. It's an older blue and white Town Car. An older one....before they got pudgy. I couldn't see much through the dark windows, but the man has a full head of hair.... not cut short like those policemen."

"Where was he parked?"

"Come over here." Mona led the way to a point in front of Snapper's door. She pointed past the elevator shaft to a parking lot of the town houses across the street. "Right in the front corner."

"Why do you think he was watching me?"

"You're the only one around here that has ever drawn that much attention."

Sage thanked Mona and continued his loading.

When the group assembled in the evening, Sage relayed the

information from Mona. "If that Town Car shows up again, I want to find out who's driving it. I have a feeling that might be our killer. If that guy is actually watching this unit and not trying to catch his wife in an assignation, we may have our man."

At sunrise Sage was up watching the parking lot, but no Town Car showed up. Just before 10:00 am Sage checked again. He made the rounds of the condo looking at all the views of Snapper's unit. He found no watchers. Sage put his Elph in the leather belt pouch so he'd have a camera in case they could spot the car. The Elph had only a 3x magnification. That would have to do.

For this trip Snapper chose his Jeep. "When we get through with the States Attorney, I'm going to dump my stash of money at the ranch."

As the Jeep approached the east garage door, Snapper punched the door opener. The Jeep passed out of the garage gloom directly toward morning sun. Ahead there was a small yellow flash. Snapper yelled "Yellow Boy" and jerked the Jeep to the right. Just as the right front fender smashed into the rear of a parked car, there were the combined sounds of crumpling sheet metal, the heavy boom of a large caliber gun, the smashing of glass and a grunt of pain from Snapper.

Before the Jeep had completed its rebound, Sage was grabbing the door lever. He glanced to the left at Snapper, who was bailing out of his side. Another slug smashed into the Jeep. Both Sage and Snapper tumbled out onto the black top. Sage was behind the Jeep and trunk of the parked car. Snapper fell into the open parking lot in plain view of a blue and white Town Car that was parked in such a manner as to point directly toward the condo. As Sage rose to look over the trunk, he could see the Town Car's driver door was open and a man was aiming a rifle over the door.

The man touched off another round, which screamed off the pavement. There was another grunt from Snapper just before a throaty roar came from the other side of the Jeep.

Snapper's return fire hit the door, smashing the rolled down glass. The door was slammed into the rifleman. He staggered back against the car. As Snapper fired his second shot, he yelled, "Wee

Willie, is that you?" The second round found the left shoulder of the assailant spinning him down to a knee. He was still able to lever a new round into the chamber and fire.

Snapper was on his feet advancing toward the Town Car holding a pair of single action revolvers in front of him, alternately firing them.

The next rifle bullet knocked Snapper to the ground. He struggled up and continued his advance. The gunman was now down, writhing about.

Sage scrambled to his feet and ran, bent over, down along the line of parked cars until he was beside with the Town Car. The assailant made an attempt to reach his rifle. Snapper fired again and again. Each shot hit its target.

Although he hadn't been counting, he figured Snapper must be out of rounds by now. When the old rancher hobbled over to stand over the rifleman, his revolvers were hanging down by his sides.

The downed man still had the strength to snarl, "You bastard."

There was one more shot. The assailant flinched another time before ceasing to move. Snapper sunk to his knees. Sage rushed to grab Snapper and ease him into a sitting position against the Town Car.

Snapper was a bloody mess. The first shot through the windshield had apparently creased a neck muscle. Another shot had hit in the left side. A third went through the meaty part of the inside of the right thigh.

As Sage was examining his friend, Golem appeared at his side. The carver pulled off his T-shirt and tore it into pieces for compresses.

A hint of a smile came through the grimace on Snapper's face. "Meet Wee Willie. I remember him now." Then Snapper slumped into unconsciousness.

Sage glanced toward the condo. The gunfire had brought out all the inhabitants to stand on the open ends of the walkways to look down over that parking lot. Mona Hatfield was waiving a cell phone, yelling in her wispy voice, "I called 911."

Wee Willy was out. He was also a bloody mess, leaking blood from wounds in the left shoulder, right elbow, right and left knees, both thighs and between his legs.

Sage grabbed his Elph and started snapping pictures as fast as he could. There was a siren rapidly approaching. He took multiple shots of the participants and the Town Car before dashing to the Jeep for a series of pictures of the initial assault. He was recording the trail of blood Snapper had left, when a Cocoa Beach car pulled up. A uniformed female officer, who had never failed to pass up the donut box, crawled out yelling at Sage. "You can't do that. Give me that camera."

Sage snapped a picture of her and said in a low voice, "You touch this camera and you'll be plastered all over the internet as an incompetent split-tail on an ineffectual police department. How would your chief take that? Why don't you go care for the wounded and dispatch your duties so you can garner high praise for your efficiency and timely performance of duty."

It only took a moment before the representative of the Cocoa Beach Police Department was rushing to the aid of the wounded. Sage followed in her wake, taking pictures.

Ro arrived at that moment. Sage removed the memory chip and stuck in a new one before tossing the camera to her saying, "You now have a story."

More sirens were coming. The police officer was at her car calling for backup. Sage pointed at Ro and said, "She's with me. Don't mess with her."

An ambulance arrived. The paramedic looked at the scene and began his labors on Wee Willie. Sage said, "This one first. He's the good guy. The other will be scheduled for a lethal injection shortly."

While everyone was fussing over the wounded, Sage started the Jeep and disengaged it from the parked car. The female cop started in his direction. Sage waggled a finger causing the cop to turn her attention back to crowd control, which was growing as inhabitants of various condos got word about the wondrous event that was occurring in their midst.

Sage backed the Jeep into the garage. He pulled up in back of Dreadnought long enough to jerk out the rear seat of the Jeep and sequester it in his car along with the used memory chip. Then he drove back to the scene and parked near the blood spots.

By now it was well past 10:00 o'clock. Ro had gotten pictures of the entire rescue operation. Sage sent her and the camera back to the condo with the instructions to call the Beach Shanty and tell Arty the meeting was called off and he should get to Cape Canaveral Hospital to question the probable killer, currently known only as Wee Willy.

Hours later, Sage was able to escape the incessant, irrelevant questions of the controlling legal authority, which had little or no knowledge of the implications of the explosive events that had just taken place in its jurisdiction. Sage gave a bare-facts account of the event without elaborating as to how it applied to significant allied cases.

Eventually, Sage, Golem and Ro settled down in the condo. A call to the hospital netted little except that the condition of the pair was not life-threatening. Sage called Clay to give him the news before the grandson picked it up on the local media. He also called Hack to report that it appeared the serial murderer had been identified and was now holding down a hospital bed.

Since no visitors would be allowed until the next day, Sage mixed margaritas. Golem opted for beer. Sage was jubilant until Ro pointed out that there was no indication that Wee Willy was the serial killer. He may have been an old enemy of Snapper's.

Sage couldn't be deterred. "I'm willing to bet that that's our boy. Despite his full head of hair, he appears to be old enough to date back to the first murder. Wait until tomorrow. Snapper will be able to explain all of this. In the meantime, I'd better call Tinna to tell her we've been delayed again."

Sage, Ro and Golem had trouble getting by a titanium-assed head nurse, who was blocking their way to Snapper. Finally, Sage called Snapper on his cell phone. Snapper passed the word along to admit the group.

Snapper's shoulders were elevated and he was wearing a cannula for oxygen. He smiled as the trio filed into his private room. He explained he wasn't breathing too deeply because one of the .45 slugs had ricocheted off the pavement to do nasty thing to three ribs. The other bullets had punched holes in meat without hitting bone.

"Before you run out of gas or that nurse chases us out, what is this all about?" said Sage.

"The moment I saw the yellow flash of the receiver of the Henry Yellow Boy rifle, memories came flashing back."

"When I was a kid, there was a young hand, a tad older than me, hired to work cattle. All I can remember is that he was named William and that was what he wanted to be called. I didn't like him much even though we were near the same age. One of the things I noted about him was that he never cleaned up when the rest of the guys were getting ready to go to town. He always went alone to the showers we'd rigged up by the lake.

"One day I walked in on him and found out the reason for his modesty. He had a pecker the size of a little kid. Of course, I broadcast the fact by calling him Wee Willy in front of the other guys. When he came to the ranch he had a Yellow Boy rifle. That gun had a distinctive brass receiver. He also had a fancy Indian blanket. Dad wouldn't permit guns in the bunkhouse, so Wee Willy left it in the main house. I'd forgotten about him owning the blanket, but the gun brought it all back."

"How long was he at the Circle K?" said Sage.

"Not long. He quit the same day I saw him in the showers. He was furious."

"Where'd he go after leaving your spread?"

"He was at the Braxton ranch for some time. He was big and tough. Before long he fought his way into the foreman's job at Braxton's."

"Out," snarled the nurse. "You've been here too long. He needs to rest."

As a parting shot, Sage said, "Ro and I will be heading home tomorrow. We'll keep in touch."

On the way out the door, Sage and company ran into Arty Misconi, who was losing a battle with Snapper's nurse.

"She says to come back in two hours. You guys tired him out. How come you're always ahead of me?"

Ro flipped her long ponytail around. "Try long red hair. It works for me." With a laugh she led the way down the hall with her little-girl skip she'd developed for an earlier adventure. Sage and Ro headed back to the condo to pack again. Sage was anxious to get back to the Hacienda.

Epilogue

Three weeks after Sage and Ro returned to the Hacienda, a large envelope from Florida arrived. The return address was Snapper's but the contents had Golem's creative fingerprints all over it. There were formal engraved invitations for Sage, Ro and Tinna to attend a private showing of Sage's Trompe-L'Oeil painting a week hence. Airplane tickets and reservations at the Courtyard by Marriott, which was within walking distance of the condo, were included. Golem was to pick them up at the Orlando airport.

Tinna was delighted to have been included on the guest list. Periodically, she was in a panic over what she should wear. She admitted that she was leaning toward going all feminine, to which both Sage and Ro expressed their unanimous disapproval.

"Figure out what goes with cowboys boots," said Sage. "That's the Tinna that Snapper is expecting. The invitations said 'informal'."

Ro's comment was "I have my size and red hair. You have your size and your cowboy boots. We use what we have."

Golem met the trio and piled them into Snapper's Caddy. Golem was intimidated by Tinna. They could look each other in the eye, but Tinna was twice as broad and didn't have knobby knees.

Sage and company were dropped at the hotel with the admonition not to eat, since drinks would start at 5:30 and dinner would follow. Golem would pick them up fifteen minutes early.

Snapper was in the foyer greeting people. He appeared to have recovered from his injuries although he didn't do much twisting.

"Sage, in half an hour the sun will be in just the right position to show off your painting. Hi Ro, it's a pleasure seeing you again. And would someone please introduce me to this fascinating filly?"

Sage did a double-take. Tinna was actually blushing. She had chosen boot cut riding pants and a blue blouse to match her eyes.

She must have adjusted the shirt while standing in the entry. It was hiked up and the tips tied under her bosom exposing considerable skin. Her hair had been poofed up to more conform to her breast shape.

"Snapper, may I present the Albuquerque voice, Miss Tinna Gunnsteindóttir or Gunn for short.

Snapper waived off the rest of the introductory liturgy saying, "She probably has more information on me than she needs. I'm Snapper. I so enjoyed our conversations. If I were fifty years younger, I'd call Sage out to get rid of him."

To Sage, Snapper said, "The light is almost right. I'll show the ladies to their seats. There's a bartender in the kitchen. Would you get drinks for them?"

"I want one of your margaritas," said Ro.

Tinna smiled at Sage as she took Snapper's arm. "You know what I want."

Not wishing to offend the young bartender, Sage said, "I have a special order." He fished around in the liquor cabinet until he found the Cointreau. As he was salting the glass, he spotted Mona Hatfield heading for the door.

Since Snapper was occupied, Sage opened the door. "Mona, good afternoon. Nice to see you."

"I have an invitation," stated Mona with pride. "I'm the only one in the whole condo to get in tonight."

"You should be. You were a great help."

Mona dropped into a conspiratorial whisper. "My walks aren't nearly as interesting as when I could spy on the spies."

"I'm taking orders for drinks. What would be your pleasure?"

"What are you having?"

" A martini."

"Me, too."

Sage passed Mona on to Golem while he fetched the drinks. When he made it to the living room, he found the chairs had been arranged in a crescent facing the painting. A space had been left in the center for the sun to shine through. However, at the moment the evening rays were being blocked by the same hurricane shutters Sage had used to keep prying eyes out. The dining room was in deep shadow.

Sage surveyed the guests. Nearly all the seats were full. He recognized everyone except one woman, whom he took to be Clay's mother and a couple.known only to Snapper. Two of the three remaining seats were soon claimed by new arrivals, Jake and Hack.

Snapper made a general introduction to the group. "Folks, these are old friends, Arn and Phil Ruck. It was their house, ID and Lexus I used when I went into hiding. I'm glad you could make it down for our little shindig. We are still one short, but that invitation was always problematical."

Snapper motioned to a young fellow whom Sage recognized as a waiter from Jake's. He had taken up a position in the master bedroom doorway.

Then Snapper stepped in front of the dining room. "Friends, please join me in raising a glass to my artist friend, Sage Grayling, who took my wish and turned it into reality. He argued that I didn't want one of those Trompe-whatever it is paintings because it doesn't hold up when viewed from around the dining table. You see, I don't care about that, because tonight will probably be the only time food will ever be served here, but nearly every night I'll sit out here or on the deck and I'll be able to see where I was born and lived nearly my whole life."

Snapper raised his glass. The assembled folks did likewise. There was a babble of greeting such as "Hear, hear, Sage, great work." Sage acknowledged the salutes with a tad of embarrassment. Tinna beamed but it was probably more at his discomfort than at the toast.

Continuing on, Snapper said, "I have another debt to Sage. He was one of my staunchest supporters in my recent problem and through his continued actions; he kept the pot boiling until I could throw this little party. There were a lot of others who helped, but I want to give a special thanks to Sage".

Again there was a salvo of greetings.

With a signal to the waiter, Snapper said, "Now it's time to enjoy my wonderful painting in Florida's golden light." The boy pressed the button and the shutters began to rise, flooding the dining room with vibrant light. Sage's painting came alive. A buzz broke out and fingers were pointed.

It was a gratifying reception for Sage. Both Tinna and Ro gave him hugs.

After the distant viewing, guests wandered into the dining room to examine the mechanics of Trompe-L'Oeil painting.

Arty Misconi was pointing at the Cad Red Dots on the chair blanket, when he called to Sage. "These were the dots that gave us another suspect?"

"Yep," replied Sage.

Snapper picked up the story line and shortly the guests were grouped around to hear his yarn.

Ro held up her empty margarita glass. The bartender and the young waiter had abandoned their beverage duties to bring the food up from the garage. As Sage was mixing a new margarita, he glanced out of the kitchen window. David Burke was standing on the walkway obviously debating on whether to advance or retreat.

Sage immediately went out the front door catching Burke by surprise. Sage stuck out his hand. "Glad to see you could make the showing of my painting." While still shaking hands, Sage broke inertia, getting Burke heading for the door.

Haltingly, Burke said, "I have an invitation, but I didn't know if I should come. Is Miss Rojas here?"

"Yep, I'm mixing a margarita for her. You'd better have a drink in your hand. What's your pleasure?"

"Do you have another margarita?"

"Sure. In a moment you can deliver Ro's. I also have to mix some martinis."

When Sage returned to the group, the smell of cooking meat reminded him of how hungry he was. Tinna was also watching the electric grill on the patio. Sage had to make the rounds accepting congratulations from the assembled guests. Snapper and Burke were standing together without fireworks, listening to Ro make an animated point. As Sage joined the group, Ro was saying, "You're still going to get a few lumps for your bullheaded initial investigation, but I won't be nasty."

"I can handle that," said Burke. "Because I listened to what you had to say at the Cowhunter Saloon, I'm trying to go in another direction....discrimination cases."

"Congratulations," said Ro with feeling. "I think you'll like a change of scene."

"You know this whole affair started out as a discrimination case," said Burke as he glanced at Snapper.

"What do you mean?" said Ro."

"If you'll give me a bit of time after dinner, I'll tell everyone how the case stands. There are three or four people I don't recognize, but all the rest have some investment in this affair."

"Everyone here, except the food crew, had some involvement," said Snapper.

Snapper had moved tables and chairs onto the deck to accommodate everyone except Jake, who brought his own bench. The dinner call sounded as the chef started laying out platters with thick, sizzling New York Strips hot off the grill. The rare ones were first. And those who wanted cremains had to go to the end of the line. Electric roasters of baked potatoes, iced bins of salad and warmers with French rolls were line up on a table along the wall. Another table held condiments.

There was no prearranged seating. Ro led Burke to the large coffee table in the living room. She pulled a couple of cushions from the couch for seats. That way they didn't have to worry about getting their chins above the table.

When the meal wound down, Snapper rapped on his glass. As silence descended, he said, "Down through the years, I've prided myself on being pretty self-sufficient, but recently it became apparent that there are times when that is not enough. Two of my most ardent champions were new friends, Sage and Golem. Thanks guys for following your instincts and never wavering. I want to tap into that loyalty one more time. I had Hack change my will leaving you two the ranch house—that ranch house," said Snapper as he motioned to Sage's painting. When I'm gone, that little chunk of land will be yours to do with as you wish. I hope that my tiny sliver of Florida history can be preserved in some manner so that future kids can see what life was like back in the early days. And thanks everyone for your assistance."

Snapper turned to David Burke, who had come out onto the patio and perched on the arm of a chair. "I also want to say to you, Dave, that faced with the evidence that was available early-on, I'd probably have come to the same conclusion you did. I'm not sure I would have continued to be as hard-headed as you, but you were certainly doing your job. No hard feeling on my part. In fact, I'm a lot better off today than I would have been without those trying times. You're welcome at my table anytime."

Burke, who was seldom at a loss for words, seemed to take a moment to organize his thoughts before standing. "Thanks, Snapper, for your kind words even though I don't think I earned them.

"I would like to amplify one of your remarks about being better off today as a result of this episode. I definitely am. This condition was brought about in large part by my confrontation with Miss Rojas at the Cowhunter Saloon. She showed me how to deal with my size in a productive manner instead of fighting it during all my waking hours.

"This brings me to an announcement. I will not be running for reelection as States Attorney." Burke smiled. "Don't be shocked. This doesn't mean I'm going to run for governor or any other public office. Ro, Miss Rojas, pointed out that as a public official, I'd always be a low-paid, little short guy.

"My intention is to take a position with a law firm in Georgetown and show my worth through my brain instead of my height. I'm working out a deal to handle discrimination cases. Thank you, Ro.

"Now, I'm going to ask Arty Misconi, a very able and long-suffering Deputy SA to tell you anything you want to know about

William Wesley, our serial killer. Arty, you don't have to worry about preservation of evidence. I'm certain this will never go to trial. However, this doesn't mean I want all the gory facts to become common gossip. All of you had a stake in the affair so this is for your personal information."

As Arty stood up, Ro produced her miniature recorder from somewhere and laid it on the table in front of Arty. Burke started to object, but when Ro gave him a sweet smile, he shrugged and settled back. Arty cleared his throat and took a sip of wine before starting. "As you know from the newspaper reports, our man is named William Wesley. He once worked on the Circle K and way back then he owned the Yellow Boy rifle and the Indian blanket with the Cad Red Dots, as they have been called. In his developmental years Wesley bulked out into a fine muscular specimen. However, something went wrong and he never developed genitals beyond those of a small boy. He was very self-conscious. When Snapper caught him in the showers and broadcast that fact, Wesley moved on. He went next door to the Braxton spread. Once he knew the ranch routine, he used a shelter for cowhunters during roundup as the site for his first murder. Two murders were committed while he worked there. He used a farm truck to pick up hitchhikers, overcome them and sneak them onto the ranch through the cattle pens that Keel and Braxton jointly owned. Originally, he used horses to carry the bodies onto the Circle K for burial. There is a slightly higher, dry ridge that comes from that side.

"Down through the years, Wesley worked in gyms and then became a personal trainer. That way he could watch males without having to reveal his deficiencies. He moved to Georgia and started his own business, a fitness gym. Every few years, watching wasn't enough. He used his vacation time to tour US 95 until he found a kid that appealed to him.

"After he moved off the ranch, he used a pickup to move the bodies and more recently he used an ATV."

"The trophies?" prompted Sage.

Arty glanced around the room. Although he was obviously uncomfortable, he continued. "Wee Willy, as everyone seems to call him, slashed all the genitalia from the boys in one vicious cut. Most of his victims eventually bled to death. His trophies went into jars of preservative. He kept a driver's license or some piece of identification with each jar. That's how we finally identified most of the victims. All the victims' clothing was burned and anything that wouldn't burn was chucked into the Indian River. The trophies were buried in a box on the Braxton ranch."

"Has Wee Willy been cooperative?" asked Ro.

Burke fielded that question. "Snapper really did a job on Wee Willy. Out of ten shots from that brace of Peacemakers, he hit the car door twice. Six went into major joints and one cleaned out his crotch." Looking at Snapper, Burke said, "You missed once."

Snapper shrugged. "Actually, that last shot was a flinch. He called me a bad name. I guess I need some more time on the range."

Everyone laughed.

"It boils down to the proposition," continued Burke, "that Wee Willy is almost completely immobile. He has the use of his right arm. A .45 slug into a joint tends to freeze it solid. He'll never be out of bed on his own again. When he's not drugged, he's looking for some way to end it all. There's no reason to hide anything now, so he keeps me awake with graphic horror stories."

When Arty sat down, little discussion groups started to form. Burke came over to take a vacant chair by Sage. "I'd like to know what you're going to do with those drawings you did of me. They're cruel."

"Oh, you've seen them?"

"About thirty times a day. My dear friends thought I should see what is being said about me. I was getting multiple copies from phone cameras over the internet."

"They served their purpose and I have no intentions of pursuing this matter further," said Sage.

"How about in Ro's ebook?"

"The story has shifted. I would imagine the thrust will be on Wee Willy."

Ro had come up behind the two men. "Unfortunately, you have been down-graded to a minor role. Wee Willy will be the star."

"Good, I'd hate to have any negative publicity precede me north," said Burke with an obvious look of relief.

As the party was beginning to wind down, Sage spotted Mona in need of assistance back to her condo. "Hi, Mona, May I have the pleasure of escorting you home?"

"Why thank you, young man. I'm afraid I couldn't keep up with you with martinis."

"You're not supposed to. Look at the difference in our body weights."

"Could you get me into the bedroom without turning on any lights? If a light shows, the phone calls will start coming in. I won't get any sleep tonight."

By the time Sage returned, a general exodus had begun. Jake was supervising the cleanup. Snapper was engaged in "good-byes." Tinna and Ro were huddled together waiting for him. Snapper slapped Hack on the back before turning his attention to Sage and company. "I'll see you tomorrow and then all this fluff will be over. I'll be having some of the local stud-horse aristocracy in. Maybe you can drum up some new business."

"That would be nice," said Sage, "but I hope nothing comes up too soon. I need some time at home. Besides, Ro and I have a lot of work to do on the new ebook. There are a bunch of photos that need work."

"It will probably be hectic tomorrow night as well," said Snapper. Since you don't fly out until afternoon the next day, let's, the five of us, have breakfast together before Golem takes you to Orlando."

ISBN 978-0-9820044-7-0